*****

"A bittersweet look at friendship."

—*Booklist*

Coach Tez patted his shoulder, then squeezed. To Simp it looked like a good grip. If it was too tight, Rollie's face didn't betray any pain. "Ay, we a team. A family. We hold up for each other," Coach Tez said, before letting go. "We ain't gonna let you slip. Right, Simp?"

Eager to please, Simp nodded, then forced himself to speak with confidence. "Got that right."

Coach Tez winked at him. The warm tingle that usually made Simp's spine feel like he could jump a mile high if Coach Tez wanted—'Rauders All Day—wasn't there this time. 'Cause Rollie was saying the right stuff, but Simp didn't believe him. And if he didn't, no way Coach Tez did.

*****

PAULA CHASE

DOUGH BOYS

GREENWILLOW BOOKS

AN IMPRINT OF HARPERCOLLINSPUBLISHERS

Dough Boys
Copyright © 2018 by Paula Chase

The text of this book is set in Garth Graphic.
Book design by Sylvie Le Floc'h

Library of Congress Cataloging-in-Publication Data

Names: Chase, Paula, author.
Title: Dough boys / Paula Chase.
Description: First edition. | New York, NY : Greenwillow Books, an imprint of HarperCollins Publishers, [2019] | Summary: Told in two voices, thirteen-year-old best friends Simp and Rollie play on a basketball team in their housing project, but Rollie dreams of being a drummer and Simp, to impress the gang leader, Coach Tez.
Identifiers: LCCN 2018052590 | ISBN 9780062691828 (pbk.)|
Subjects: | CYAC: Basketball—Fiction. | Best friends—Fiction. | Friendship—Fiction. | Gangs—Fiction. | Brothers—Fiction. | African Americans—Fiction. | BISAC: JUVENILE FICTION / Social Issues / Friendship. | JUVENILE FICTION / Social Issues / Adolescence. | JUVENILE FICTION / Family / Alternative Family.
Classification: LCC PZ7.C38747 Dou .2019 | DDC [Fic]—dc23 LC record available at https://lccn.loc.gov/2018052590

20 21 22 23 24 PC/BRR 10 9 8 7 6 5 4 3 2 1

First paperback edition, 2020

 Greenwillow Books

*

*To those who are judged
before they're truly seen and heard*

SIMP

On Monday, Wednesday, and Friday he was a sucker, 100 percent—sitting in the house waiting on his boy Rollie to get home from his talented and gifted classes like he couldn't haunt the streets of Pirates Cove on his own.

He could. It just wasn't the same.

Deontae "Simp" Wright's four younger brothers fussed over the video game they were playing. Even Little Dee, who was only two, clamored for the controller, and all he knew how to do was push buttons and freeze the screen in the middle of a play or turn the game off just as somebody was ready to score. Their screeching got on Simp's nerves.

"Ay," he yelled, staring at 'em.

Derek, the seven-year-old, closed yap. Dre and Dom, eleven and nine years old, muttered under their breath. Simp didn't retaliate. Muttering meant they respected him enough not to come out of their face wrong.

Most days he played with 'em. But he was too keyed up waiting on Rollie. They were supposed to run a little ball when the rec opened for free play at seven. The twin, Chris, would probably be there too. Dude had only lived in Pirates Cove for six months, but he acted like he was all that just 'cause he could rap and sing.

Before Chris moved in, all Rollie had cared about was balling. Now all he talked about was playing the drums. And it wasn't like he ain't play drums before. Shoot, he was always banging on something and coming up with new beats. But once Chris moved into the Cove and started talking about how the TAG program was gon' help him get put on in the music industry, it was like all of a sudden Rollie thought that was gonna happen to him, too.

A hundred million people was out there trying

get put on to rap, sing, or be in a band, and these two fools was acting like being in some little after-school program was gon' put them in front of super producers or something. It was crazy to Simp.

He wasn't trying to dead Rollie's dream, though. That was his boy. He just wished Rollie would remember there was other stuff out there important, too, like balling with the Cove Marauders and trappin' for their coach, Juan Martinez. Shoot, trappin' for Tez was even more important than balling 'cause they got paid for it.

Dough boys doing their thing, Simp thought with a big grin.

He knew that technically all him and Rollie were was lookouts. At least for now.

Simp was the one that got them put on. He was the one who Coach Tez had approached with "What's your name, little soldier? You good with the rock. I think I need you on my team . . . you and your little partner."

Coach Tez ain't mess with dummies. And low-key, it was one of the reasons Simp had agreed so fast to hustling. Everybody thought Rollie was the smart one just 'cause he was always all quiet and serious. Nobody ever told him he went too far saying what was on his mind.

Whatever. Closed mouths didn't get fed. Simp couldn't help that he told stuff like it was. He wasn't trying hurt nobody's feelings, but he hated how everybody always acted like they had to find a polite way to tell the truth. The truth was just the truth. Coach Tez trusting him with the rock, on and off the court, was proof that he wasn't as dumb as people thought he was, even if his nickname gave people the right to assume that.

And that was thanks to his mother and one of her trifling boyfriends. One day Simp didn't move fast enough when she called him so she yelled, "Get your simple butt over here, boy." After that, ol' dude was always, "Ay, little Simp, come here." He had only been maybe five years old. Ol' dude was long gone. The nickname never left. Simp never tripped off it. Hood nicknames had a way of sticking, especially when it was your own mother who gave it to you.

It didn't help that he had failed sixth grade. Then he had to take summer school that next year to get into seventh. It didn't make him dumb. School just wasn't that important to him. Not like basketball. Or making paper.

Still, one of the reasons he let his massive head full of locs dangle down his face was 'cause it helped hide that his hairline looked like somebody had taped it too close to his eyebrows. It made it seem like he was always squinting, trying to figure things out. He couldn't help that. People was gonna say what they was gonna say about him.

All he knew was once him and Rollie joined Coach Tez's basketball team, they also was part of his hustle, first as errand boys, now as lookouts working the front. Dumb could get you hemmed up by the police. So, trust, he wasn't dumb one bit.

Working the front made Simp feel like he'd swallowed electricity. To anybody else they just looked like they were chilling out front near the entrance of the hood. But they were watching, signaling to the runners that cars coming in were either all right or leecee. Sometimes, when more than one cop car rolled through they'd slink away, separating as they whistled or hooty-hooed. He never wanted nobody to get caught up on his watch. He loved knowing he had the runners' backs.

Now he wanted to be one of the dudes Coach Tez trusted the most. He just had to keep it up.

Naw, *we* gotta keep it up, he thought.

Him and Rollie were a team, and if they did it right, they could be heading a crew—with five or six dudes doing the work for 'em—by the time they were sixteen.

Him and Rollie each got 60 dollars every time they worked the front. So Simp knew crews had to make big bank. That's where he needed to be. At thirteen, he was the oldest and had to help take care of his brothers. He was the one who taught them how to handle their business at the bus stop or school if somebody stepped to them. He was the one who made sure they got something to eat. Shoot, he was even the one who picked up Little Dee from the bootleg babysitter, Ms. Pat.

Her house always stunk like crappy Pampers and something burnt. He hated how five or six kids was always playing some game whose only rule was run and scream. Dee was even starting to join in. All he knew was if somebody ever hurt Dee, he was gonna go off. He told his mother they should put him in a real day care. Hint, hint—one near her job so she could do pickup. But she had hit him with "And who paying for a 'real' day care, Deontae?"

He had started to say he would. 'Cause he definitely

could have helped. But he didn't need her knowing how much money he had.

The memory of the first time he handed his moms a stack of bills filled him with warm purpose. She had side-eyed him. "Boy, where you get this money?" And before he could stop the words, he'd said, "Don't worry 'bout it."

He had steeled himself for the smack coming his way. Instead his mother, Niqa, had stood there for a few seconds staring at the ball of scrunched-up bills he'd handed her. Then she'd sniffed and said, "Hmph, how your little peasy head gon' tell me not to worry about it. I worry 'bout what I want, Deontae . . . but, thank you." She'd kissed him on the cheek and walked off. It was the closest she ever got to saying he'd done something right.

Now he slid her money regularly and they had an understanding. She ain't ask where he got the money and he ain't tell her. She still went upside his head every now and then, talking 'bout "Don't go thinking you grown just 'cause you give me some ends now and then, boy."

But that was for show. He saw how her eyes always got wide when he passed her some money. And then once she came to his room, standing at the door, her mouth pursed like she was mad but her voice gentle, "Deontae, you got a few dollars? I need get Dee some Pampers."

He'd reached into one of his shoeboxes and pulled out thirty dollars like it wasn't nothing. And it wasn't. He had money stashed in different places throughout his bedroom, hidden from her and his brothers.

"This good?" he'd asked, the bills fanned out in his fingers.

Her eyes went from the bills to the box. She nodded and plucked them out of his hands. What Simp remembered most was how she stopped at the door and said, "Thanks, baby," before she walked away.

That's what was up. He was taking care of his. His mother got on his nerves, always expecting him or Deondre to watch their younger brothers. But the fact was, he'd do whatever he could to help her keep the lights on. Rollie ain't have brothers to chase after, toughen up, or feed when they got hungry. Maybe that's why he had so much time to daydream.

All Simp was really good at was basketball and counting. Playing for the NBA would be cool, but it wasn't nothing he thought about all the time, like Rollie did music. Real talk, he had a better chance of being like Rock Jensen, one of Coach Tez's top earners, than LeBron. That was messed up. But it was real. And he was about the real. Rollie could go 'head and daydream.

His brothers was a pain but he loved 'em. They would never be hungry or get punked by anybody if he had anything to say about it. And on that he was the last word.

He checked the clock on the cable box.

5:00 p.m.

Thirty more minutes and Rollie would be home. He stood up and pulled one smartphone out of his right pocket and another out of his left. The two phones looked almost exactly alike, except his real phone was in a shiny silver case with his basketball number, 8, emblazoned on the back. He got it made at one of the stands in the middle of the mall. The dude had said it was real silver. Big ballin', baby.

The other, a burner phone, was in a simple black case. The front was cracked like it had been dropped a few times. It was always on or near him, in his pocket or under his pillow when he slept—just in case his coach sent a message. He threw it on the coffee table, sat back on the sofa, and toyed with the idea of texting Tai, the only other person from their squad who wasn't in TAG. But he didn't know what he'd say and whatever he did say she'd probably be all, "Simp, why are you texting me?" Just like that. Not "y u texting me" but full-out "why-are-you-texting-me?"—writing out every word like he was too stupid to understand any other way.

Tai was always giving him a hard time. He played it off like he ain't care, but the more Tai put him down, the harder he worked to make her like him. Every time he wanted to be like *man, forget her*, he'd think about her in a pair of tight jeans hugging her curves like they loved her and he'd be right back laughing at anything she said or agreeing with her when she went off about something.

He forced his fingers away from her number and instead recorded himself lip-syncing. It was his favorite app and one of the only things that passed time while he did what he did all the time lately: wait on Rollie.

Dom gave him a look. Before his mouth was barely open enough to form a sound, Simp smacked him in the head. "What, you got jokes?"

Dom turned back to the game, glossy eyed but wordless and without tears. "That's what I thought," Simp said.

Secretly, he was proud of his brother for not crying.

The burner phone skipped a few inches across the coffee table as it buzzed. He grabbed it just before Little Dee's chubby fingers enclosed the phone. He checked the text as he scooped Dee into his arms to head off his wailing.

10.10

"Gimme, Thimp," Little Dee demanded. He squirmed, reaching for the phone and kicking to get down at the same time. "Lemme see."

"Stop, man." Simp squeezed him tight. Dee behaved but kept reaching. Eyes on the coded message, Simp dropped him gently onto the couch, ignoring his outstretched arms.

He texted back *9* and grabbed a knit cap.

"Dre, watch everybody till I get back. I need make a run."

Deondre sucked his teeth. "Mommy ain't home yet. You can't leave till she get home."

"Don't be telling me what I can't do," Simp snapped. Babysitting was wack. But he had to go. "Look, if

Mommy ask, tell her Coach called for me."

Dre's lip drooped. Simp couldn't blame him. He'd always hated when their mother would rush out the house with some half-ass instructions, never saying how long she'd be gone or even where she was going. Worse, when something went wrong—and it always did with boys running wild—she went upside his head like it was his fault he was only nine years old and couldn't stop his five-year-old brother from leaping off the sofa and cracking his head on the entertainment center. And that was before Little Dee was born. Now, half the time, between Derek and Dee, it was like running a day-care center.

Being shackled to his brothers was what it was, and Dre was next in line for the cuffs. "Yo, look, you second-in-command. Just hold it down." Simp dug in his pocket and pulled out a twenty-dollar bill. "When Mommy get home, you, Dom, and Derek walk up to the Wa and get y'all self something. All right?"

Dre's eyes lit up. "All right." He stuffed the money in his pocket and let Little Dee crawl into his lap.

"I want a chili dog from the Wa," Dom said, never taking his eyes off the game.

"Can I get a slice of pizza?" Derek asked, pumping

his fist as his character on screen pummeled Dom's.

"You gon' have to ask Mommy. Ouno if she cooking or not," Simp said. He knew she probably wouldn't. But dinner wasn't his problem, right now. He grabbed his jacket, anxious to beat feet. "Dom, Derek, help Dre watch Little Dee. Hear?"

There was a chorus of "yeah"s as Simp zipped his jacket. He turned his back on Dre's stony face. If it had been any other message, he would have waited for their mother. But it was a 10.10—get here soon as you can. No telling when his mother would show up. She got off work at five but that ain't mean nothing. She might get in at six; she might get in at eight. Making sure her older boys took care of her younger boys was the only rule Niqa Wright enforced on a regular basis.

Dre would be all right, Simp told himself.

He let the cold air clear his head. It wasn't even five thirty and the streetlights were already on. It was still people out. Some called out his name, throwing up a hand or fist in hello.

People was always out in the Cove. Even three-bedroom rows weren't that big inside. To stretch out, people milled out on their stoops, found reasons to linger around their cars talking, or started dice games under the streetlights.

The Cove had eleven courts—all named by the alphabet, like whoever had made the community didn't think it was important enough to give the streets real names. He lived in fifth court. But the hood was deep, every bit a mile. And once you got past fifth court, everybody called 'em by their letter. He guessed it sounded crazy to say you lived in eleventh court.

His legs took him past the three basketball courts and the rec center into the Kay. Most times people didn't go beyond the rec center when they visited the Cove, leaving the Kay forgotten and, low-key, forbidden. It was backed up by an even thicker band of woods than the front of the hood. If you walked far enough through the trees, there was a ravine that fell off into a small stream.

Any and everything went down in those woods. People hung out near the Kay to do their dirt 'cause if you didn't live in that court, it felt like you were doing something in private. That was hardly true in the rest of the Cove, where news spread quick.

More fights broke out in the Kay than any other court. Mo was the only one in their squad who lived in the Kay. She always had something to say, like she wanted you to know she wasn't the one to mess with. Also, Mo stayed forever on his case. But, low-key, he had mad respect for her. It wasn't easy living on the street that had such a bad reputation that even the police didn't bother with it unless it was bad bad. Like murder bad.

It was where Coach Tez's main girlfriend lived. Where he spent more time than at his own house. Where Simp had been summoned by 10.10.

As he got closer, he took a few deep breaths to get his pounding heart under control. You never knew what Coach wanted when that 10.10 came through.

His mind went down a quick list—had they let the wrong car through last time they worked the front? Had Simp missed an earlier call?

He wondered if Rollie had gotten it, too. Maybe they were ready to get their crew. Simp already knew what he wanted it to be called—the EC Boys, named after the courts him and Rollie lived on. Plus, EC sounded like easy, so people knew they was so good they was chill.

Maybe it was finally time for the EC boys to run game.

Still, he knew better than to assume anything with Coach Tez.

He counted the doors as he walked past, forcing his mind to be blank. He came to door number seventeen, a green door, and knocked.

ROLLIE

If there was anything better than a pickup game of basketball, Rollie wasn't sure what it was. The scraping of everybody's sneakers as they started, stopped, and hustled around one another trying to get their shot off had a beat—*scut, scut, screeeech . . . pat, pat, pat, pat*. Their hard breathing made a cloud of wispy smoke in the cold January night, before disappearing up into the lights illuminating the court.

Then there was the *ting* of the ball as it hit the ground, only broken up by somebody's "man, get that outta here," or "ay, ask about me" when the ball sailed over everybody's head and satisfyingly sank into the net.

Five of them fought for the right to score. Every man for himself. Your point was your own. Just like missing was your own. As long as you could take some teasing over missing a shot, nothing was at stake if you lost. Only one person could win anyway. So at least you weren't a loser by yourself.

Rollie loved it. Even in the cold he loved it. Pickup ball always cleared his mind. After every game he'd go home with a new beat he wanted to tap out on the drums. He didn't know why the two were connected, but they were.

He successfully shot a jumper, scoring three, then raced back down the court ready to steal the ball like it was his alone. Simp had the ball. His little brother, Dre, was already waiting under the basket, crouched like he would tackle whoever crossed his territory. It made Rollie smile. Dre was eleven, the youngest of the rest of them, but when he played he meant business.

Aight, you want play with the big boys . . . let's go, Rollie thought.

He barreled toward him, swiveled so his back was to Dre, and boxed him out, determined to take the ball from Simp. They were tied up. If Simp scored, game was over. If Rollie got the ball back and scored, game was over.

Dre bucked up against Rollie, unafraid. Rollie had to go up on his toes to stop from tipping forward. In that instant, Dre darted around him, swiped the ball from Simp, and was down the court before anybody could defend him.

"Yo, your boy got the quickness," Cappy said to Simp. His breathing was ragged.

Simp beamed. The single platinum cap on his front tooth gleamed. "He got a little something going."

Rollie took the opportunity to race past them, rebound Dre's shot, and take it in for an easy layup. He laid the ball on the ground and pronounced matter-of-factly, "Game."

"Man, Cappy, you messed me up. I had this game," Simp said. But he didn't seem upset, for real. He put his hand out to Rollie and they gripped fingers then pounded each other on the back. "Good game, son."

Rollie felt like putting his hand to his ear and asking for the crowd to roar. It was so good running up and down the court. The sounds of the game pushed him even harder, like basketball was its own mixtape. But he took his friends' congratulations in stride, murmuring thanks as each of them gripped his hand.

"I catch y'all later. I got homework," Chris said, peeling off with only a good-bye nod. Chris was cool with Rollie but still an outsider to everybody else. Him and Dre were the only two playing that weren't already on the Marauders team. In the beginning, everybody played him harder to see if he could take it—elbowing too much, shoving to see if he'd shove back. Once he'd proven he could give it as good as they gave it, it settled in like a normal game. But Rollie wasn't surprised Chris wasn't interested in another. He was most comfortable making up rhymes and song lyrics.

If this had been 'Rauders practice with all the drills, sprints, and yelling by their coach, Rollie would have felt the same way. But he was up for another game.

After everybody grabbed their sweatshirts, Rollie, Simp, Cappy, and Dre stood huddled mid-court talking.

"Man, I ain't gonna lie. Shawty had me out here ready pass out," Cappy said. "I know you trying out for 'Rauders come April. You got the goods, son."

Cappy gave Dre a congratulatory pound as if he'd won. He was the Marauders second string point guard, backing up Rollie, and had a bad habit of always trying to impress Simp. It annoyed Rollie. It was like Cappy was always trying to be him.

But Dre's teeth shone so bright he looked like he'd swallowed a light bulb. Rollie felt bad for denying him the compliment.

"Yeah, I want to," Dre said, looking to his older brother for approval.

Simp smacked him lightly in the back of the head. "He all right. I guess he 'Rauders material."

"Can we run another game?" Dre asked. "I was ready catch up to you and Rollie."

"You thought it was," Simp said, scowling. He picked the ball up and tossed it, hard, at Dre. "Let's go."

Like that, the game was back on.

That was the thing about street ball, you ran with the pack or walked off the court. Rollie fell into the rhythm. Sweat glistened on his face and his hot head steamed in the cold air. In no time, him Simp and Dre were tied up. It was game point. He didn't usually talk trash, but the occasion seemed to call for it.

"Everybody that's ready for this tail whipping, say yeah," Rollie said, his smile teasing.

He bounced the ball on his left, then his right, taking the time to catch his breath.

"Oh, yeah," a voice from the sidelines hollered.

"That's what I'm talking 'bout. The rec center closed but look at my boys out here balling like they know what's up."

Rollie froze inside.

It was their coach. Rollie knew Simp and Cappy were probably thinking the same thing—anything they were planning to do before had to be stepped up. He saw it in the eager way Simp crouched lower, hunger in his eyes like the ball was his first meal of the day; the way Cappy straightened up gulping air to keep his chest from heaving. Even Dre seemed to eye the ball more intently, his limbs twitching ready for the reach in.

When their coach was around, "ball so hard" wasn't a suggestion; it was a demand.

Coach Tez was about five foot four, only two inches taller than Rollie. His arms were toned, but he wasn't muscular at all. He had light brown eyes that always felt like they were staring into your brain. He kept his hair in a complicated style of freshly done cornrows—usually zigzags, loops, and circles. One time he'd even got the team's name spelled out in the small, neat braids. On the outside he looked like an ordinary pretty boy, not like somebody that could command an operation of hustlers.

But Rollie knew better. He didn't know for sure how big Tez's crew was (and didn't want to know if he was being real), but they held down the Cove and another hood, Monarch's Way. Streets claimed Tez was trying to take over Del Rio Crossings. Rollie figured if Tez wanted the Crossings, he could take it. But it was probably just a rumor to keep the two neighborhoods beefing.

Tez wasn't no joke, though. If he fixed you with a look and talked in a voice that never raised unless he was coaching, you listened. Rollie liked it better when he yelled. When he didn't, some sort of punishment followed. Having him appear for a pickup game could only mean two things: one, he wanted to be entertained as they battled one another to win or, two . . . dough boy business.

Rollie wasn't in much of a mood for either.

Of all the times, why had he picked that moment to trash talk? Now if he made the shot and won, Tez would be pleased. Which was fine, Rollie guessed. Lately, he wasn't sure which he feared more—Tez praising him or scolding him. Working hard had a way of turning on you, with Tez. But Rollie went for it.

He took a breath, pounded the ball hard on the court

to get the blood running back to his fingers, then juked right as Simp reached in. He was clear to the basket. He took the jumper, certain it would go in, when Dre leaped up like he had springs in his shoes and snatched the ball out of the air.

Rollie was still staring at the spot Dre had been when the scurrying of everybody's feet and Tez's exclamation of "Yooo, look at little dude!" reached his ears. Him and his crew, Rock Jensen and the 'Rauders assistant coach, Monty, exchanged dap. They all clapped it up like they were at a real game. Tez waved them to the sideline. Everybody jogged over. Rollie lagged behind a step.

If Tez hadn't been there, losing wouldn't have mattered. It was just a game.

Except when Tez shows up, he thought, shame heating his face.

He snatched his skullie off the ground and smashed it down onto his head, wanting to disappear into it.

They all stood around Tez as he talked about hustle and heart. He dapped Dre up three times, congratulating him for outrunning dudes who "should have been faster and stronger" than him. They all felt the dig and kept their eyes respectfully downcast.

Rollie pretended he was learning. Pretended that he was listening and that next time Tez saw him on the court, in practice, he would do better. He tried to make his nods as solemn as Simp's, his eyes as wide with admiration as Cappy's, his smile as grateful as Dre's. He was doing the motions, but he didn't feel any of it.

All he had wanted to do was play some basketball tonight. Play some ball, then go home and air drum whatever beat rolled around in his head, so that when he got to his TAG session he could play it and maybe even get Mr. B to record it, so he wouldn't lose it.

That's all he wanted.

He didn't feel like being coached. Or schooled.

He didn't want any knowledge dropped about winning big and hustling hard.

And he definitely didn't feel like hearing Tez weave in and out of talking basketball and hustling like the two were one. Because at some point, the talk would come to that. It always did.

But he was trapped. Everybody around him was all "yes, Coach" so he parroted it, speaking up when they did. The sounds of the court slowly died in his head. Whatever beat had been building disappeared and was replaced with the firm, preaching of their "coach."

The next day Tez's words still rang in Rollie's ears. But not for long if he could help it. The second he began beating on the drums, he could forget. And if he couldn't forget, he could at least drown it out. Sticks up, hovering over the drums, he waited on Mr. Benson's signal.

Mr. B always looked homeless in his khakis and oversized sweaters. A hair pick, the real old-school kind with a fist at the end, swam in the middle of his uneven choppy bush. The clenched jet-black fingers of the pick bobbed in his sea of coarse silverish hair. And his beard couldn't decide what color to be. Most of the week it was splotched with patches of gray, then by Monday it was black again.

On the streets Mr. B would have been an easy mark. But inside the music room, he played drums like a beast and zoned out anytime somebody got the beat "just right." Watching him jam to somebody's groove made Rollie feel like drumming was air and Mr. B was breathing in every note. Watching somebody enjoy his playing filled Rollie's chest so much he thought he would float to the ceiling. He kept his eye on his teacher, ready to set it off.

Mr. B stood in the middle of the room, one hand

up in the air, the other on the mouse of the laptop. Once the hand came down, his left finger would tap the button and the dull click of the metronome software would start.

Keep beat with it or die, Rollie told himself, hands already sweating from gripping the drumstick.

It wasn't that serious, but it felt like it. In group sessions, some people hated timing drills. Anytime Mr. B yelled out "You're a beat behind" or "You're too far ahead," there was always at least one person who argued the software's click was wrong. Not Rollie. He had three beats in his head at all times, so once Mr. B set the metronome, he was ready. Every now and then the 'nome won. But most times he got a "Good job, Roland."

Getting that "good job" was the best part of his day sometimes. Better than sinking a three in basketball. Better than getting a good grade in science, his worst subject. Better than anything. And he didn't care if that was corny.

One time he had thought being in the talented and gifted program would make him seem soft. Like some band geek. Sure enough, the auditions over the summer drew every nerdy marching band drummer within twenty miles of Del Rio Bay. Part of Rollie knew he could play just as good as any of those cats. But another part of him wasn't so sure. Then he'd made it into the program, met other dudes who felt like the instrument they played was a part of their body and Mr. B, who talked about music like it was a religion. Now Rollie wasn't sure how he ever got through a whole day without talking nonstop about beats, kick, rim shots, and riding.

Mr. B's hands came down in a flash.

Rollie waited—one, two, three—on the fourth beat he kicked into gear.

Boom boom chickah chickahboom chick
Boom boom chickah chickahboom chick

His foot hit the bass drum while his right hand, crossed over his left, flicked at the cymbal making the sound he wanted. He kept time with the 'nome, letting it tell him when to flick vs. kick.

He loved the boom of the bass drum. Even Mr. B called it the sound of the party starting. Depending on where you were, either you were gonna tap your foot or shake your butt.

The beat rose through Rollie's feet and into his arms as he stung the cymbal, firm enough to get the *ting* he wanted but not so hard that it rattled out of control. He boomed, tinged, and tatted until Mr. B's hand shot up. Rollie breathed hard and ragged, energy coursing through his limbs.

Mr. B beamed at him. "You're definitely getting better. You're not forcing it as much. That's the secret." He sat down on top of the only other real furniture in the room, a steel-gray desk, head nodding like Rollie's beat still played inside it. He glanced into a folder. "Are you still playing at church?"

Rollie gulped back his racing heart. "I play once a month on youth Sunday." He admitted almost apologetically, "I don't think my grandmother gonna ever let me stop doing that."

"So, you have school, TAG, the church band." The folder smacked closed. Mr. B's eyes studied him. "Anything else?"

Rollie's senses spun like a compass out of control. He'd spent the last four months juggling TAG and balling for the Marauders. Coach Tez was already losing patience with him coming to practices late. He didn't need somebody else questioning his loyalty. His answer was slow and reluctant. "I play basketball. You know, for a select league squad."

"I could have guessed that," Mr. B said. "You live in Pirates Cove, right? I balled there when I was your age." He seemed amused at Rollie's pop-eyed surprise. "I wasn't great. But I grew up in Del Rio Crossings, so we used to come over there and ball. It wasn't an organized team or anything. Just guys getting together to hoop and claim which hood had the baddest players." He folded his arms and frowned. "It wasn't as territorial between the hoods back then."

The turf war between the Cove and the Crossings was bad. And it wasn't over no street ball game, either. If Mr. B was from there, he probably knew that.

Rollie automatically looked down at the one newish-looking thing on his teacher, a pair of well-polished burgundy loafers with shiny pennies in them. Mr. B hadn't been on the streets in a long time, probably. So maybe he didn't know.

As if reading his mind, Mr. B chuckled. "Surprised I'm from the Crossings?"

"A little," Rollie admitted. "You come off like a band geek, that's all."

"I probably did back then, too. I never had the same cool as the guys that played ball." His chin lifted in defiance. "I still knew how to play a little, though. So, which one you love more? Balling or music?"

Rollie's drumstick drooped and sent a gentle *ting* waving. He clamped the cymbal between his fingers. One thing that probably hadn't changed since forever was how quick stuff got back to the hood. If Mr. B still had people in Del Rio Crossings, it could happen easy. He didn't want to be real and answer "Music," then have Coach Martinez question his loyalty to the Cove or the Marauders.

Mr. B was at the platform beside Rollie's drums in a few steps. "It's okay if you like 'em both. Or if you don't know. If you play ball half as good as you drum, then it's probably hard to pick between two things you love."

Rollie took the sucker's way out, nodding and letting his teacher believe what he wanted. The thing was, he didn't love playing for the Marauders anymore. When it had been just basketball he did. Even when it was basketball and a couple random favors for Tez, he still liked it. But it wasn't neither of those anymore. It had grown into a job that Rollie hadn't applied for.

The knowledge of his secret dealings burrowed deep into his head, hiding. He laid the drumsticks down and forced his hands to lie still on his lap. They itched to play more so he wouldn't have to talk about Tez or balling.

"You taught yourself how to drum. So did I, and I recognize raw talent," Mr B. said. He tapped absently on the rim of the bass drum. "Since you're in TAG, I'm gonna assume you love music enough to put in the work to get better. Am I right?"

"Yes, sir," Rollie said.

"Good." Mr. B pulled a folded paper out of his back pocket and held it inches from Rollie. "There's something I want you to consider. If you decide to do it, I want to help you get ready for it. If you don't" —he showed his palms— "no harm, no foul. So only say yes after you think about it."

Rollie watched the slip of paper come near him then jerk away.

"Probably silly for me to share this and expect you to keep it a secret." Mr. B's smile said he knew it was pointless. "I'm going to say it anyway: keep this to yourself. The Rowdy Boys are looking for a drummer." He chuckled. "Based on the look on your face, you've heard of them."

"They're the only go-go band from Del Rio Bay to get a record deal," Rollie said. He cleared the rasp of awe out of his throat. "Everybody know 'em."

"Yep, well, that record deal is a little on hold right now," Mr. B said. "The drummer left the group and they're trying to keep it quiet, hoping they find a new one before the record company washes their hands of the whole mess."

Rollie managed to rip his eyes away from the paper. His mouth dropped open. "You want me to audition?"

Arms folded, Mr. B looked Rollie up and down like it was the first time he'd thought about it before confirming, "Yes. That's exactly what I'm proposing." He put his hand up, stopping a nonexistent interruption. "You need to understand it's a long shot. You been drumming for what, six years?"

"Yes, sir. Since I was seven," Rollie said, still unbelieving. He'd seen every TRB video and not just the ones that went viral once people caught on that there was a local boy band on the come up. He'd even been the first to click through and comment on "Jam That Jelly." He still remembered his post: Swaggy.

B-Roam, the lead vocalist and hype man, had thumbed up the comment.

He went back to the video all the time to see how many people had jocked the comment and liked it. It was up to five hundred. His brain could barely compute being inside one of those videos, jamming inside B-Roam's family room or wherever they shot them. There really wasn't any "used to" about it. He still low-key stalked their videos when they dropped. They had signed a deal a year ago. Everybody, including him, had been waiting for a single to hit the radio. Now he knew why it hadn't.

A streak of pleasure at knowing the inside scoop gave him that light, airy, floating feeling. He squeezed his knee to force his attention back to Mr. B's voice.

"Normally, six years would be a raindrop in an ocean when it comes to getting to the next level. But go-go bands are about raw talent, and that you got." The paper tapped the bass drum with two firm clicks. "And at this point, you have as much experience as the other band members except for maybe B-Roam and Money Mike. I think they're both fifteen."

"Sixteen," Rollie confirmed. Knowing that made him a stan, probably.

"Long story short, I know the band's manager and I told him I'd keep an eye out for prospects. I was ready to tell him no go. But I like how you handle the skins." Mr. B's eyebrow raised. "They probably have a lot of people trying out, secretly. But you're the right age for them and even if you don't get selected, the audition process is the best way I know to help musicians grow. So—" He stretched the paper out, shaking it lightly at Rollie. "Take this to your mother. If she has questions, we can talk. And if she approves, we'll talk about arranging some private lessons to get you ready for the audition. Cool?"

Rollie couldn't feel the paper between his fingers. He was sure Mr. B said more, but he didn't hear it. With a robotic "See you later," he left the room, then immediately opened the paper to see what magic it held. It was only some type of permission slip, but to Rollie it felt like a ticket to another dimension. He folded it neatly and slipped it smoothly into his jean pocket for safekeeping.

SIMP

Everybody's house had rules.

Rollie's mother (well, mainly his grandmother) made sure he never missed church. Even during basketball season, on Sundays, he had to roll to church and either get dropped off to the game after or miss it since it seemed like church people loved having a morning and afternoon service.

Bean ain't have no mother that Simp knew. But her father, Mr. Jamal, had hella rules. Low-key, Simp was scared of Mr. Jamal. He was always on a mission to stop people from rolling through the Cove to buy drugs. He was one of the reasons Coach Tez started using more 'Rauder players as lookouts—'cause Mr. Jamal was calling the cops on the older dudes left and right.

Cappy's mother was even more strict. Simp had forgotten to take his hat off in her house one day, and she straight went off on him about how disrespectful it was. How it was a shame nobody cared about manners anymore. She lectured him until Cappy reminded her they were gonna be late for practice. It was probably only about five minutes, but to Simp it felt like forever.

All his friends' parents had rules.

But ain't nobody have rules like Niqa Wright. 'Cause at least with other people, you knew what the rule was: go to bed at ten or clean your room before I get home. It was never that simple with his mother.

Him and his brothers had learned early that to keep the peace, everything was about not making their mother mad. Which was hard 'cause just about anything made her mad.

I beat your butt if you come in here crying.

I beat your butt if the school call and say you been acting up.

I beat your butt if you break something in the house from playing too much.

From where Simp stood, crying, acting up, and

playing was probably the three things little boys did best.

His mother wasn't that big, and at five foot six Simp had caught up to her in height. But his mother had the hardest hands he'd ever felt. When she slapped, she reared back so far, her hand disappeared behind her head. When she pinched, it felt like a sharp claw trying to wrench your skin off. Still, Simp wasn't afraid of her anymore. The minute he'd given her money and she'd looked at him like he'd just saved her life, he had stopped being afraid. As long as he'd been lacing her with cash, she hadn't hit him a single time. Yeah, she still threatened and got that look in her eye when she was mad, but she didn't hit him.

So why did his shoulders jump when her face, eyes narrowed, mouth a thin line, suddenly appeared in the bathroom mirror?

He scowled, more to hide that she'd scared him than anything. "Dang, Ma. How you just creeping up on me like that?"

She leaned on the doorframe, arms folded. "How I'm creeping in my own house, boy?"

He left it alone. Even though she hadn't whaled on him in a while, he wasn't trying to make her homesick for throwing hands on him. He adjusted a gold sweatband around his head, taking his time sliding it into place. When she saw he wasn't going to answer, her mouth lost its tightness.

"This job on my last nerves," she said, combing her fingers through her long straight weave.

Simp's first thought was, What that got do with me?

His mother was a receptionist at a doctor's office. She answered calls all day and signed in patients. Sitting on the phone didn't seem all that hard to him. He forced his face to stay neutral and muttered, "Um-hm."

Her words poured in a stream of steady rain.

"Youno what it's like, Deontae, out here trying provide for five hardheaded boys." She paused, eyebrow up, daring him to challenge the statement. She swished hair off her shoulder, like she was mad at it. "And it's bad enough I'm dealing with rude and nasty patients all day. Now they talking about wanting to add more duties to my job." She rolled her eyes. "But oun hear them talking about more money. They make me sick with that mess."

He reluctantly turned away from the mirror and leaned against the sink, gripping its sides like it was every day him and his mother stood in the bathroom chatting about her job. His mother didn't do random conversations. She wanted something. Even though he just wished she'd get to it, his stomach swerved with uncertainty.

"On top of that, everytime I turn around, y'all outgrowing your clothes." Her lips pursed at the thought. "And my raggedy-ass car acting like it's ready go up on me. That's the last thing I need."

Before the stack of problems grew any higher, Simp finally asked, "What? You need money or something, Ma?"

Her head reared back as she laughed, but when she looked at Simp her eyes were sharp and curious. "Why? You got money?"

He sucked his teeth. "Ma, don't play. I'm serious. You need hold something?"

"Hold?" She snorted. "That mean I'd pay you back. I'm your mother. Either you gon' give me what I need or youn have it. But I ain't borrowing nothing from you. Shoot, I'm still the one paying the rent up in here."

Anger bloomed in Simp's chest. How was she turning this on him like he'd said something wrong?

He sucked in a breath, held it for a second, then

let it out as he asked, "I'm just saying, did you need something?"

She smiled. "If you got something."

Her and all this blah-blah she was talking, like she had to prove she needed money, confused Simp. Usually she didn't have no problem just asking. He rushed her along.

"Ma, I got go practice. Can you just tell me how much you need?"

Her lips pursed. "Oh, so you the parent now 'cause you giving me a couple dollars?"

Simp slid past her in the doorway and headed to his room, across the hall. He put his 'Rauders jacket over his black hoodie. The hall was small enough for her to stand in the bathroom doorway and still talk to him. She was fussing but the edge was gone. "I need, like, two hundred. You got that?"

Her voice went up a notch on the question.

He smirked to himself. He had it. "I might. But I'mma have to look when I get back."

"Um-hm, 'might.'" Bitter doubt edged her words. "How much money you hiding around this house, Deontae? Oun care where you put it. You know if I find it, in *my* house, it's mine."

He knew she meant it, and he couldn't fight the heat rising in his head. All she had to do was ask and he'd give it to her. But naw, she had to be extra and remind him that she ran things. Things that he helped pay for.

Since he'd been hustling, he'd helped pay the cable, the electric, and even some of the rent. He squashed the urge to point that out.

He kept money in all types of places—taped under his desk, behind posters on his wall, even behind one of the little outlet plates. Sometimes hiding it was a game, just to see if he could find a new way to do it. Each time he'd go back for the money, he half expected it to be gone. But it was always there. His brothers knew better than to go into his room without asking first. If it ever disappeared, he'd know it was his mother.

Up until now, it had felt like they had a deal. He kept giving her money because she'd never taken it without asking. It showed she respected him.

Now she was acting like him helping her out wasn't nothing. Or like he ain't do nothing to earn it. It was never enough with his mother.

Simp stood in his doorway. His jaw clenched as fear and anger boiled in his gut.

He fixed his mother with a blank look. "I ain't hiding nothing. But it's my money. I work just like you." His heart pounded as he waited for her to step to him, palm open ready to slap.

Lips pursed tight, her eyebrow went up a notch. They both stood their ground for a few seconds before Niqa's laugh trilled in the dim hallway. "Um-hm. You might work, but you don't work like I do." She called over her shoulder as she walked away, "Leave the money on the table for me. I need it by tomorrow morning."

All he could think was, Why couldn't she just ask for the money and keep it pushing? He would have said yes, no matter what the amount was as long as he had it. But she had to go and punk him. Then she ain't even say thank you.

He wasn't even worth a thank-you. That hurt.

All he could do was take his anger out on the basketball.

Ping.

Ping.

Ping.

The ball smacked against the wood then hopped

back up into Simp's palm, like the floor had spanked it. All around him *ping*s jumped off as the team warmed up, but all he heard was the sound of his own ball. He cradled the rock in one hand. Then turned it slowly, feeling its tiny bumps. They made his fingers tingle. Got 'em ready.

He was a beast on the floor. Could see what moves had to be made to get the shot off in his head. Knew exactly how hard to flick his wrist to get the ball through that extra space to get to the basket. He didn't have to work hard to be good at basketball. It was why becoming a Cove Marauder was his destiny. They were the best select team in the state.

The Cove also had a recreation league ball team, the Cougars. Anybody could play on that team. No tryouts. No cuts. It was just something to do after school for most dudes. The 'Rauders were different. You worked hard to make the team, and once you did you'd do anything for your teammates. They were in the battle with you, every game, mowing down the opposition.

Even among other great players, Simp was special.

The year he tried out, this dude had bet that Simp would score at least fifteen in the scrimmage. Everybody thought it was a sucker bet. At eleven, Simp was skinny and just under five feet tall. No way he was going to outscore the taller, stronger boys. But he had. He'd scored twenty-six points, and the dude had won a hundred dollars. He'd slid Simp twenty.

He'd known then exactly what being a 'Rauder meant. It was everything to some people. Dudes from ten years ago were still talked about as if they'd just played a game. He wanted that love. He wanted that power. The only thing missing was his boy.

He bounced the ball, letting its magic sink into his digits as he watched the door anxiously. TAG ran later on Fridays. But Rollie should have still been here by now. If he was coming.

Simp slammed the ball to the floor to block out the spidery nerves building in his stomach. Rollie needed to come on. He was ready mess up if he didn't bust in that door before Coach Tez.

'Rauders All Day wasn't just a motto; it was a pledge. One they all took when they agreed to play. That included practice and making your shift for working the front. Rollie was starting to slip.

Simp dribbled, hoping to quiet his worry.

Ping.

Ping.

Then a whistle screeched.

Coach Tez stood in the middle of the court decked out in a black velour warm-up suit. It was zipped down just enough to show a fresh bright white T-shirt. He rocked a pair of black slides with the tiny symbol of a slam-dunking Michael Jordan shining out in white. From across the gym it was hard to tell, but the flip-flop on his right foot had a slightly thicker sole. All of Coach Tez's shoes did—custom-made to hide his limp.

Streets claimed he'd been shot. But it was only a rumor. Simp didn't know a lot about their coach, but he did know Tez had been hurt in a construction job a long time ago. He'd heard his mother say a thousand times she wished she had it like Tez—"out here collecting disability and barely paying any rent 'cause he 'can't work.'" She always said it with her lip upturned, like she didn't believe he was really hurt. But her eyes was always dreamy, like she wished it was her.

If he was faking, he was good at it. Without the special soles, Coach hobbled more than he walked. The only time he limped was when he stood too long. But it was just the start of practice. He was ready to go. He blew the whistle again, letting it shrill longer than he had to.

Simp cast one last look at the door just as Rollie jogged in, out of breath, stripping off his hat and jacket as he crossed the gym floor.

"You pushing it man," Simp said through a huge grin. He put his hand out and Rollie gripped it in a shake. "Few more seconds and you woulda been doing sprint drills by your lonely."

"I couldn't get out the house. My moms was fussing because I forgot to do the dishes," Rollie said breathlessly as he undid his warm-up pants in one motion. The snaps made a tiny clacking sound. Simp and Rollie walked over and joined the team.

With his boy next to him, Simp felt like he could run the world. He listened, holding on to every word Coach Tez said, ready to will his body to do whatever was asked.

Practice broke into full swing.

The team was run like an army with Coach Tez as the big general and Simp as the little one. It didn't matter that there were a few older dudes on the team; whoever Tez knighted as the team's general was the general. Period.

The big general yelled his command and Simp enforced it.

A blow of the whistle meant either stop or go. Get confused on which it meant and they got extra drills: sprint and rebound drills, layups until their legs were noodles, dribbling and juking street ball–style to see how fast they were at keeping the ball away from one another.

It went on like that for an hour, then right into a scrimmage against one another—no matter that the "warm-up" would have been practice enough for any other team. They weren't any other team. They were the Cove Marauders, five-time 'Peake champions.

The Chesapeake Invitational was a three-day tournament with the top twelve select teams competing to be state champ. At this point, every team was playing for third place. The 'Rauders and Pumas battle for one and two had left the competition littered all over the court. If Coach Tez had anything to do with it, they'd never lose their dominance. The entire season was about the 'Peake.

Captains didn't get picked until a month before the 'Peake. Starting five was juggled and tweaked specifically with 'Peake domination in mind. They could be undefeated the whole season, but lose at the 'Peake and the team caught trouble.

Coach Tez bragged on their five wins so much that, at first, Simp thought they got money or something. But their number one ranking and the four-foot tall, fake gold statue were the only payment he'd seen.

By the end of practice, the gym was hot and humid and the floor slick from the team's sweat.

Coach Tez put his arms up and shouted, "Bring it in."

Some of the boys, their legs exhausted, took their time getting to the huddle. Simp jogged over like he was ready to go more. When he reached the huddle first, he was rewarded with a clap of the shoulder. He kept the grin off his face as he listened intently.

"All right, y'all looking pretty good out there." Coach Tez scowled at Reuben, who had enough sense to hang his head. "But some of you look like you tired. What you tired for? If you was a pro, all this—even the scrimmage—would just be the warm-up before a practice."

Simp straightened up at that. He mean-mugged Reuben.

"I need y'all to look at these next few games like it's the championships already." Coach Tez scoured the circle of sweaty dudes, piercing each one with a look.

When he made eye contact, the player was expected to nod so Coach Tez knew he understood. "We gotta secure first place at the J. Martins Tourney. That's the first time we really get to see what our competition look like before the Chesapeake. If we walk away ranked anything less than first, don't even matter if y'all can climb out that hole at the 'Peake. Oun want nobody thinking we soft. Ya' heard?"

There were mumbles of "yeah," "yes, sir," "yes, Coach."

Coach Tez smiled. "Good. Y'all got a target on your back, whether you like it or not. Everybody gon' be at the J. Martins trying scope out our game and keep us from the top spot." His voice rose with passion, giving Simp goose bumps. "Play big, win big. Anybody slack at the tourney and you getting benched." Simp gulped as Coach Tez side glanced at Rollie. "Ain't nobody's spot safe. Believe dat." He stretched his hand out into the huddle and the team did the same, piling on top. "'Rauders All Day, on three. One, two, three . . ."

"'Rauders All Day!"

The chant bellowed throughout the gym. While it echoed, the players scattered, talking and laughing. They rushed to get dressed. If Coach Tez hadn't asked them to stay, no one ever lingered.

The two players with the slowest drill times, Cappy and Squirt, started putting the balls away and mopping up the sweaty floor. They worked fast with their heads down, ashamed of the duties. Every week somebody had to do it. It was inevitable. But nobody liked coming in last. Having to clean had the stench of loss that you couldn't get off you until the next practice when somebody else skunked on their drill.

Simp stayed by Coach Tez's side. He watched Rollie chat up J-Roach and Reuben, then nodded toward the cleanup crew. "We got wait for them finish or you ready talk to us now?"

"They know what to do," Coach Tez said, walking off.

Simp grabbed his stuff and threw it in his duffel without getting dressed. He strode, long legged, behind Coach Tez. He looked to make sure Rollie was right behind and was relieved when he was.

Nobody talked while they walked to a large shed behind the rec center. It was only an equipment shed, but let people tell it, it's where Coach Tez kept all his money from hustling. Simp had never seen evidence of that, but he'd never done nothing to stop the rumors.

Only 'Rauders players were allowed in the shed. He liked that people was always guessing at what was real and what wasn't.

The shed was bigger inside and cleaner than some row houses. The gray wood panels and door framed in white wood made it look like a miniature version of a house you'd see in the country. Except it didn't have any windows and was only one big space inside. A space that was bigger than his bedroom. He'd never measured it, but he was good at counting and guessing at distances. His room was small. Five steps in and you were at the back of it. The shed was definitely bigger— at least twelve steps to the back, maybe more. Every time he came out to the shed, to put equipment away, he thought about what it would be like to have all that space to himself.

Coach Tez took a key out of his pants pocket and unlocked the heavy-duty lock that kept the doors together. It was both a storage area and Coach Tez's office. The other rumor was the walls were bulletproof. Simp couldn't see anything special about the walls. They were plywood. Not even painted. But anything was possible with Coach Tez.

On one wall, shelves were stacked neatly with

basketballs, extra nets, and uniforms. Two short file cabinets were against the back wall behind a wooden desk that sat in the middle of the shed. There was a chair, plush black leather that looked too fancy and out of place on the concrete block floor. It barely fit behind the desk.

Coach Tez plopped into the chair and nodded at two folding chairs, the only things leaning against the third wall of the shed. Rollie handed Simp a chair. They unfolded them at the same time and sat, quiet.

Coach Tez's teetered back and forth. He steepled his hands and put his thumbs underneath his chin. Simp wondered if they were supposed to talk first. He didn't know about what, though. He swallowed over and over trying to make his mouth ready when it was time to say something.

Finally Coach Tez's lips parted with a tiny pop. "You know, I can't figure y'all out."

The words made Simp's nuts crawl into his stomach. He hadn't expected to hear anything like that. He was barely breathing as Coach Tez went on. "When I recruited y'all, it was 'cause I thought y'all was a team. You was always together so—" He shrugged. "I ain't usually wrong about people. But maybe this time, I was."

Simp wanted to shout, "No, you wasn't wrong. We a team. Ride or die." But a small part of his mind knew this was part of the game. He kept his eye on Coach Tez and remained wordless.

After a few seconds that ticked on like eternity, Coach Tez leaned his elbows on the desk, looking from one to the other. He burst out laughing, and the sudden sound made Simp's shoulders jump. "I ain't gonna lie, y'all some tough little bastards," Coach Tez said. "Even some grown men would have confessed to a crime they ain't commit after too much quiet. Relax, little soldiers. Relax."

Simp's shoulders sagged. He turned his mouth up into what he hoped was a smile. There were two small knocks and one thump on the door—'Rauders signal. He was so on edge it took a deep breath for him not to jump at the sound.

"Come in," Coach Tez said, eyes on the door.

Squirt walked in with two big netted bags full of basketballs. He walked them over to a hook on a wall, securing them so the bags wouldn't jostle, then tried to slip out. "You lock up?" Coach Tez asked, stopping him mid slink.

Squirt nodded, then seeing Coach Tez frown added, "Yeah. We good, Coach." He tried to dismiss himself one more time, then stopped again when Coach Tez's voice called out, "Ay, hustle next time. Let somebody else do the scut work."

"Yes, sir," Squirt muttered.

"Where Cappy?"

"He had to go home," Squirt said, sinking his hands into his coat pockets. "He helped. I just told him I'd bring the stuff back here."

"Let me find out he bailed and his butt gon' be cleaning up the gym after practice all season," Coach Tez threatened before waving Squirt away. He stared after the door a few seconds longer, then jumped right back into his talk. "All right, the thing is, y'all two are special. It's been a long time since I had a package deal like y'all." A smile lit his face, showing a platinum cap on his incisor. In the center was a T outlined in tiny diamonds. "The way y'all control the floor together is one of the reasons we been able to keep the streak at the 'Peake going. I ain't never think that would happen once Roman and Carlos graduated."

Simp sat up straighter.

Coach Tez had just compared them to the two best players in 'Rauders history. Both of 'em was locked up now. It had been their dumbness, though, as far as

Simp was concerned. Ain't nobody tell them to turn into stickup boys robbing convenience stores. He waited to hear the words that had to come after that: *I'm promoting y'all.*

Instead, Coach Tez's eyes fixed on Rollie. "I need to know what's up. Y'all still in it together or what?"

Simp jiggled his foot, willing his mouth not to answer. Rollie gotta soldier up on this one, he thought, at the same time praying, *Come on man, say the right thing. Please.*

Rollie's answer wasn't what Simp had hoped.

"TAG make it hard for me to get to practice on time."

Coach Tez waved off Rollie's words. "Yeah, I know. You told me that back in November. I don't mean that, though." He squinted into Rollie's face from across the desk. "I'm asking, are you still committed to the whole game and nothing but the game?"

Simp swore he heard his own heart beating. He opened his mouth, hoping to get more air in. At the same time, Rollie blew out a big breath. He slumped an inch in the chair and adjusted his skullie on his head. His voice was so low, Simp leaned his way to hear better. "Man, it just feel like too many people want something from me," Rollie said.

Coach Tez's eyes were now soft and curious. He pulled his lips in until they disappeared, pooched them out, then pulled them in again. Simp found himself sucking his lips in, too. He'd come back here thinking they were getting promoted, and now Coach Tez was questioning Rollie.

He fought the frustration rising in his chest. He didn't want to blame Rollie. His mother and grandmoms had probably pushed him into TAG. Coach Tez would work it out, though. Rollie just needed to be helped through the hustle. He breathed easy, confident it would all work out.

"I know what that's like," Coach Tez said. "I'm not trying be one of those people pressuring you, though. The work you do for me should be helping you and your family. Know what I mean?"

Rollie nodded slow, like he was in a trance.

Simp looked from Coach Tez to Rollie. The fear in his stomach settled into rabid curiosity.

"I always told you, if you not wit' it no more, you need be real with me and let me know," Coach Tez said. "You saying you want out?"

At this, Rollie's head seemed to snap up. Simp's body jerked upright like they were connected. *No, say no*, he screamed in his head.

"Ay, Rollie, I ain't gon beg you to be on my team," Coach Tez said, his voice cold.

"It ain't like that." Rollie sat up straighter but didn't raise his voice. "Naw, I don't want out."

Coach Tez walked around to where they were and sat on the edge of the desk, between their chairs. "So, something else on your mind then. You know you can tell me," he said.

"I got my moms and grandmoms on me about school and doing good in TAG. My TAG teacher trying hook me up with auditions to be in bands." Rollie blew out another breath, slumped. He folded his arms as he lifted his face up to Coach. "It just feel like a lot going on. I'm not trying slip up or nothing, just 'cause everybody all on me at once."

Coach Tez patted his shoulder, then squeezed. To Simp it looked like a good grip. If it was too tight, Rollie's face didn't betray any pain. "Ay, we a team. A family. We hold up for each other," Coach Tez said, before letting go. "We ain't gonna let you slip. Right, Simp?"

Eager to please, Simp nodded, then forced himself to speak with confidence. "Got that right."

Coach Tez winked at him. The warm tingle that usually made Simp's spine feel like he could jump a mile high if Coach Tez wanted—'Rauders All Day—wasn't there this time. 'Cause Rollie was saying the right stuff, but Simp didn't believe him. And if he didn't, no way Coach Tez did.

ROLLIE

Once Tez dismissed them, Rollie couldn't get home fast enough. And why had he mentioned auditions for bands? Mr. B had told him not to say anything. He hadn't even told his moms yet.

Worst, Tez had given him the chance to say he was done. Why hadn't he?

Every time the question raced around his brain, he heard himself telling Tez how he was still down.

Stupid. That was just stupid.

Simp's voice came from far away. "Everything all right, son?"

Rollie jammed his hands into his jacket pockets and

nodded. He didn't feel like talking.

"Look, I need keep it one hundred wit' you," Simp said. Their steps were in sync. He easily kept up with Rollie's fast but shorter stride. "Don't take this wrong but . . . was you lying to Coach just now?"

Rollie stopped dead, inches from a streetlight. In the slice of light, he and Simp stared at each other. The worry on Simp's face was the only thing that kept Rollie from going off on him.

Any other time he would be straight up with Simp, but things were getting complicated. He laughed inside at the lie. Getting complicated? It always had been. The second he held three creased and crumbled twenty-dollar bills in his hand after four hours of sitting on the fence near the Cove's entry and "whoop whooped" any time a cop patrolled, it was complicated. That was the first favor Tez had ever asked him and Simp to do. They had been in the sixth grade.

Had it really only been two years?

He knew then it was wrong. But hanging out near the entry or at center court was just something they did to pass time anyway. If Tez wanted to give him sixty dollars just for that . . . why would he have said no?

Whether they sat out there for one hour or three,

the payoff was always sixty dollars. Always in twenties. Twenty dollars an hour—more sometimes. He wasn't even sure his mother made that much, and she had been an administrative assistant at the Haven House forever.

But then Tez started asking them to do it more regular. Next thing he knew, him and Simp had a schedule. They were legit lookouts. They had the two-to-six slot on Saturdays and right after school on Tuesdays and Thursdays, unless they had basketball practice or a game.

Rollie made so much money there wasn't enough candy, pizza slices, and hot dogs he could buy from the Wa to spend it. Eventually, he started buying new clothes, then hiding them at Simp's house. He'd break out a few new items every now and then. Whenever his moms or g-ma would ask about the new clothes, he claimed it came from the rec's lost and found. If they ever checked, they'd find out the rec purged lost items every single month by leaving unclaimed clothes on a table for people to take. It wasn't a total lie.

He knew he could only do that so many times. Now he had only God knows how much money stashed in his room deep under his bed in an old duffel bag. He was scared to count it. But he was pretty sure he could help his moms pay rent a few months and still have some left over.

Complicated.

When he got into TAG, he had a plan. Play ball with the 'Rauders this last year, then quit once he got to high school. He'd seen other people do it. Most of them did it because they played ball for Sam Well High and couldn't really do both. And if that's what it took, Rollie would go out for the Sam Well junior varsity. Whatever it took to leave the 'Rauders without trouble.

Only, leaving the basketball team wasn't the problem and he knew it. Just like he knew that Tez wasn't talking about balling with all that "you want out" mess. If you wanted out from a team, you quit. Tez wasn't talking about that. And for a second, Rollie had almost answered yes. But the way Tez had grilled them, leaving all those empty spaces, waiting on somebody to spill their guts. That stopped him.

He knew two things—everything was a test with Tez and Simp worshipped him.

So, he'd lied and said he was still down.

"What I need lie to Tez for?" he said, his voice a

tick above a whisper, the tone they used anytime they talked about their hustle. He pulled his skullie down until it touched his eyebrows and held Simp's gaze.

"I ain't saying you did," Simp said. He shrugged his duffel onto his shoulder more securely, threaded his fingers over the handle to grip the bag. "Just saying you been late to practice a lot. You know Coach. Don't really matter what the reason is. He feel like if you want get there on time, you do . . ." For a second his eyes pierced Rollie. "Even if you gotta hit somebody up to pick you up from TAG instead of waiting on the bus. Know what I mean?"

Rollie only laughed to get the bile churning in his belly under control. "Is that a hint? Did Tez tell you that's what I need to do?"

Simp brushed his face with his hands. "Rollie, man, I just don't want him start questioning where your loyalty at. You know Reuben or somebody would roll out and get you soon as TAG ended. It would get you here on time is all I'm saying."

Simp wasn't wrong. Rollie knew he had to show that he was down. But wasn't he already doing that by staying on the "team"?

"I'm good," Rollie said. There was still a question

in Simp's face. Rollie let his duffel drop to the ground. He shivered a little inside the black satin Marauders jacket, a gift from Coach for winning the 'Peake. They were cool to look at but not built for warmth. "Can I keep it one hundred?"

Simp's head nodded, eagerly. "Always."

"Iouno if I can keep doing this—"

Simp broke in. "Reuben can come get you after—"

Rollie shook his head at him. He took a step closer to Simp. No one was near them, but he lowered his voice more. "Not practice, son." When Simp nodded once, Rollie went on. "It's cool that Tez think we ball like Rome and 'Los, but ain't no secret they was his top two boys back in the day."

Simp leaned back an inch like Rollie's words were a sneeze he wanted to avoid. "What's wrong with that?"

Rollie's head thudded softly. He wanted to have a real conversation about the game— about what they do for Tez. How'd they'd got in and how to get out. He also knew the first rule of the game was you don't talk about the game. Not even with a dude you'd been down with since first grade.

"Nothing wrong with it if we about graduating to

the pen." He scooped his bag back onto his shoulder, ready to get out of the cold. "I'm just saying I'm not. Know what I mean?"

"I ain't either, son," Simp said. His brows furrowed in confusion. "They was stickup kids. What that got do with us?"

"Naw, you right. You right," Rollie said, tiredly. "I got a lot going on, that's all. I don't want my game to start slipping."

"Never that. You know, I got you," Simp said. He put his fist out. Rollie tapped it with his own.

When they had first joined the team, Rollie had been with it—Tez's advice on how to keep the hustle on the low, how not to get caught. It had felt good being in the "family." But they were eleven years old then. He couldn't remember when he'd stopped believing. But he had, and he wanted Simp to see they were getting in too deep. It wasn't going to be today, though.

He wanted to tell Simp about the audition for TRB. It was their favorite band. Until TAG, him and Simp had always done everything together. He didn't want Simp to think he was bragging. Plus, it was barely real to Rollie. And it wasn't like he might really make it. Was it?

He'd tell him eventually.

He reached in, gripped Simp's hand, and pounded him on the back.

"It's all love," he said. "Late to practice or not, I'm ready to ball. We gonna roll through and take the J. Martins. Number one seed, believe dat."

Simp shouted into the air, "They knoooow."

"We knoooow," Rollie shouted back. They gripped hands and went their separate ways.

Later he sat in his room. The smell of frying pork chops flirted with his nostrils. Through the smooth jazz floating throughout the house he heard the door slam, announcing his mother was finally home from work. He forced his legs to take their time and walk normal into the kitchen where her and G-ma sat talking. The chops sat center stage of the table, a bowl of mashed potatoes and steaming string beans beside it. Normally he'd be anxious to guzzle down a meal, but his stomach was balled with even more jolts of joy than after he made TAG.

His mother looked tired, but she smiled when he kissed her cheek.

"Hey, baby." She rubbed his arm. "Ready to eat?"

"Can I show y'all something first?" Rollie asked.

G-ma shooed him. "Yeah, while you setting the rest of the table." She fanned herself like it was blazing. "I been cooking for the last hour. G-ma tired."

Rollie handed his mother the paper, then gathered plates and forks, silently, while she read over it. His grandmother's lips pursed as she waited for someone to fill her in. When it didn't come fast enough, she prodded. "What is it? He not in trouble, is he?" She gave Rollie a side-eye before focusing on the paper in front of his mother's face.

"Is this legitimate?" his mother asked, handing the paper over to G-ma. "It says that if they pick you, we need to sign a contract." Her brows crinkled. "That sounds serious."

"A contract for what?" G-ma scanned the paper with her finger. "What is this, Ro?"

He sat down across from them. They stared at him, his mother looking worried, his grandmother confused, and that's when it sank in. Mr. B thought he was good enough to try out for a real band. He could be a celebrity. His heart beat proudly as he explained. Even the disapproving head shake of his grandmother didn't kill his excitement. She said a hasty prayer and scooped food on her plate, signaling it was time to eat whether they felt like it or not.

Rollie's fork grazed over his dinner as she scolded. "I don't like this, Vernita. It's too much. He just got in this talented program." She fixed Rollie with a look. "How you know this thing is real?"

His grandmother's word was the last word. If she convinced his mother to say no, it would be no. Period. He looked from one to the other, then focused on G-ma. "Mr. B said you can call him and ask any questions you want. He knows their manager. It's not like some shady audition he just heard of from the Internet or something. G-ma, the Rowdy Boys been together since they were in elementary school. Remember the paper did that big story on them and they was on the news?"

His heart flipped when his mother's face brightened. "I knew I'd heard of them somewhere before." She scooted the paper from her mother's grip and reread it. "Harold 'Pee Wee' Jamison . . . that's their manager. He was on there with them talking about how good they were and how the boys were self-taught musicians." She laughed at that. "Ma, remember? Because you said you knew some Jamisons that used to live near center court."

Rollie jumped in. "I don't know how Mr. B know him, but maybe they grew up together. It's real, though. Mr. B connected like that, I guess."

"And how you gonna keep playing for the youth choir if you doing all this?" G-ma asked. Her teeth clanged against the fork as she shoved a piece of chop into her mouth. She chewed it for a few seconds, then turned to his mother. "He already doing too much. Playing basketball and what not. You should wait till report cards come out, then decide."

"But they trying to fill the slot now," Rollie said. He calmed the high-pitched panic he heard in his voice. "G-ma, it's just an audition. I don't really care if I make it, for real. But it would be so crazy if I didn't at least try."

He hated lying. But, if Mr. B thought he was that good, then making it wasn't so crazy. His grandmother was on some old-school stuff not wanting him to always be out there "running the streets," which, to her, was anything but going to church. That was where his mother was different. She had let him play for the 'Rauders because she thought it was better than him just hanging out on the street corner. And Rollie had never told her any different. Never planned to and wouldn't have to if he could kill the audition. If he got into the band, him playing for the 'Rauders and doing what he did for Tez would take care of itself.

He pressed his grandmother once more. "Please, G-ma? Mr. B already know I play for the church." He made a face, teasing. "I already told him you won't ever let me stop that."

The tiny wrinkles around her mouth disappeared as she smiled. "You got that right." She lightly jabbed her fork his way. "The Lord gave you that talent, and the least you can do to pay Him back is to play in church. Hmph." She raised an eyebrow, daring either of them to challenge her. When they didn't, her face relaxed. "If your mother find out this is real, then go 'head and try out. But be careful." She moved her attention directly to Vernita. "Remember when Rowena's granddaughter got caught up in that modeling thing?" She shook her head, mouth in a deep frown. "Sat there and spent all that money thinking that child was gonna be a top model or some nonsense. Then everybody running around trying help her pay her rent and light bill. It didn't make no sense."

"You know I know better, Ma," Rollie's mother said. She gave Rollie a look, and they shared a smile. "I'll give his teacher a call and see what it's about. I got a few questions anyway."

Satisfied, G-ma went back to eating. She started talking about some drama popping off at the church. For her, the conversation was done. Rollie's stomach was too full with excitement to eat, but he picked at the chop to avoid his grandmother's lecture about wasting food. He wanted to share his news with somebody. Somebody who would understand what it felt like to see a door halfway open and feel like if they just ran headfirst they could bust it open and end up somewhere good on the other side.

There was only one person like that. Mila Phillips.

He forced down the last few bites of his dinner, waited for a pause in their conversation, and asked if he could go. Deep in their gossip, his mother waved him on. He was barely up the stairs as he texted Mila:

the wildest thing just happened

He pulled books out of his backpack and stacked them beside him on the floor. He put his phone on top of the books, waiting for Mila to hit him back.

Over the summer two things had happened—one, he was kind of, sort of halfway talking to Metai Johnson, and two, he had run into Mila, in the Woods, while he was visiting his cousin Michael. He wasn't looking for a girlfriend, but he was feeling both of them. Problem was, Mila and Metai were best friends.

Since Mila was in TAG, he used it as an excuse to hit her up now and then. But real talk, he liked vibing with her. After he promised her that he'd keep their conversations on the low, Mila seemed cool with them talking . . . about TAG, at least. Once Rollie had tried talking to her about a TV show she'd mentioned liking and she went ghost on him. She hadn't answered another text from him until he'd popped up a few weeks later asking about the TAG dance recital.

It was stupid that he couldn't just talk to Mila about whatever he wanted. He had known both of them since first grade. But in Tai's mind, they were already exclusive. So, he took the hint. He didn't want them beefing over him, so he only ever hit Mila up about dance or drumming.

The smile on his face was genuine when her message came back: *what? U and Mr. B going on tour?* 😄

He couldn't help thinking how Tai probably couldn't remember his TAG teacher's name. Tai cared about what Tai cared about. And Tai didn't care about TAG or even his drumming. At least she never acted like it. He loved that Mila knew him well enough to guess something that had to do with Mr. Benson.

He sat with his back against his bed, elbows propped on his knees as he typed back: *I know this gonna sound corny but don't tell nobody pls.*

JahMeeLah: *cross my* 🖤

Roll-Oh: *Mr. B hooked me up with an audition*

JahMeeLah: *Roland that is incredible. For real for real.* 😬 👋 *so like a band that you would get paid to be in?*

Rollie basked in her excitement. It surged through him like electricity. His fingers danced across the screen: *yup. If my mother say yes he gonna help get me ready for it.*

JahMeeLah: *would she say no?* 🤭

Roll-Oh: *lol my g-ma would fo sho.*

JahMeeLah: *oh right. Granny don't play.* 😌

Roll-Oh: *say word.* 😄 *it ain't like I think imma get the gig or anything. But I can't lie, Mr. B thinking I'm good enough to try got me trippin a little*

JahMeeLah: *if he think u good enough to try then he*

probably think u could get the job tho. That's crazy. Good crazy 😊

Rollie read her words over. He was too afraid to believe them. He was too afraid not to believe them. Either way, this audition could change everything.

SIMP

Simp held the tiny white Ping-Pong ball suspended above the table. Chris stood across from him, calm. Simp wasn't fooled. Chris's eyes shifted quickly from the ball to Simp's eyes like he could gauge when it would drop. But Simp had him. He'd won points off the last three serves by just waiting.

The rec center was packed with people milling from the foosball table, past the Ping-Pong table, and to the corner where the TV blared music videos. With both game tables taken, most people piled on the other side of the room, clustered in groups talking or half playing some of the old board games. Music, laughter, and random shouts of dissing mingled together. The few days the rec stayed open until nine were guaranteed to be mob deep, once February hit, thanks to the cold and early dark. Nobody was trying to sit in the house at six o' clock like it was time for bed. But to Simp, the noise in the game room was far away. He was used to it. Even the squad sitting on the "sideline" calling out comments didn't throw him.

They had been lucky enough to get into the game room and onto the old lumpy sofas near the Ping-Pong table before the crowd. Mo, Sheeda, and Chrissy sat on one couch, Rollie between Mila and Tai on the other. The only times Chris scored on him was Simp's own fault, 'cause he'd been sneaking a peek to see if Tai was all up on Rollie. He'd considered losing against Mila on purpose so somebody else could get next and he could slip in on the conversation. Then Chris had yelled out he had next and Simp wasn't about to pass up the chance to spank him. Once he smashed the ball into his face, it would be his second win.

He faked a tremble in his hand. Chris didn't move.

Punk getting used to my style, Simp thought.

Plain and simple, he didn't like Chris. Dude acted like he was too good to kick it with anybody but Rollie.

He hadn't once stepped on the court or the rec by his self. Had never hit Simp up to chill. It was like they hadn't met the same time he'd met everybody else he seemed so close with.

Didn't matter. After Simp finished with him he'd have another reason to stay his punk butt home "writing his rhymes."

Simp's mouth pursed in concentration.

Just as he relaxed his muscle to let the ball go, Mo shouted, "Man, would you please just serve." She slammed her back against the sofa, arms folded. "Me and Sheeda would like to play, today. This getting boring."

Simp ignored her yammering, but Chris's eyes slid Mo's way for a second. When they did, Simp dropped the ball and whacked it hard. He pumped his fist as it flew past Chris's last-second attempt to jab at it.

"Sucker," Simp muttered. He threw the paddle onto the table.

"That's game," Sheeda announced, hopping up. She raced over and reached for Chris's paddle. "Sorry. Good game, though."

"It's good," Chris said. He sat next to Mila on the

little block that pretended to be a table. "Shoot, the game coulda ended ten minutes ago if Deontae ain't take five minutes between every serve."

The squad's laughter pumped annoyance through Simp's veins. "Don't be mad 'cause you got gamed, son." He thumped down next to Chrissy and pulled his cap lower to hide the murder in his eyes. He didn't need nobody knowing how much Chris got to him. They would think it meant he cared what dude thought of him. He didn't. Just didn't like him was all.

Rollie piled on. "It did stretch the game out, B."

Simp swallowed hard and forced the tightness in his throat to ease back. "So everybody hating my style. huh? Must mean I got y'all running." He slouched down on the sofa, jaw tight.

"Just jokes, son," Rollie said. "You the reigning champ."

Simp stayed looking forward, seeing beyond Mo at the table and at people clustered on the few chairs and sofas surrounding the television. Everybody was with their set, loud and joyful, happy just to be out. He should have felt the same way. But nothing felt the same anymore. They were all together but it still felt off. It had since him and Rollie's talk with Coach

Tez. He felt like he was on the outside looking in at everybody else, not knowing who to trust.

He mentally took count of where he stood.

Him and Tai were getting along better. On TAG days, she was always talking him up on the bus ride home.

And him and Rollie was still cool, weren't they? He thought so but couldn't shake it.

Everybody had eagerly agreed to hang out tonight, didn't they?

Maybe it was just him.

He sighed hard to push the doubt away as Sheeda continued the roll of apologies. "Nobody hating, Simp. But dang, we all want get a game in before they shut down for the night." She reached for and missed the ball as it lazily sailed her way. "Aww man."

"Good try," Mila said. Her big bun of tiny braids shivered as she clapped politely.

Simp caught himself rolling his eyes at her being so nice, then apologized to her in his head. That was just Bean, always keeping the peace. He knew she wanted everybody to call her Mila. She claimed she'd outgrown the nickname Bean. But she was always gonna be Bean to him.

Tai piped in. "For real, though, nobody feel like

taking a hour to finish one game of Ping-Pong." Simp couldn't see her over his brim but felt her hand tap his elbow playfully. "I'm just playing. Y'all know I don't care about no Ping-Pong. Rollie keep promising to show me how to play *NBA Extreme*."

Her touch made his insides jelly. Simp listened to her go in playfully on Rollie, wishing it was him. He'd known Tai a long time, but the last few weeks was the first time she treated him like he didn't annoy her. Much as he hated how TAG took Rollie from him, it meant him and Tai rode the bus without the crew sometimes. They were stuck with each other. A distant hope sparked in his chest.

He was about to volunteer to teach Tai whatever she wanted when Chrissy's soft voice reached him. "I suck at stuff like Ping-Pong. The ball moves too fast."

He raised his head enough to glance at her from under the cap and had the perfect view of the two small rounds poking out the T-shirt hugging her skinny frame. He stared a few seconds longer, wondering what they felt like. What his hands couldn't prove his groin imagined. He sat up straight, hoping it adjusted him so nobody saw the peak growing in his jeans.

"You play good, though, Deontae," she continued.

He shrugged. "It ain't hard. You just got stay focused."

She folded her long legs under her. "Chris tries to hit the ball too hard. I don't like that thing coming at me that fast." Only a few inches separated them on the sofa as her cushion sagged toward his. She raised her voice over the growing noise. "I like foosball though. When the table open, wanna play?"

Simp held his head back far enough to check the foosball table. Merce and Champ were in a heated game, rocking the table as they spun the silver levers too hard. He doubted they'd finish anytime soon, but he nodded agreement.

He'd never said much to Chris's twin. Had figured she was stuck-up like him. He raised his head a little more to check her face. They didn't look that much alike for being twins. She was cute, though. "I could teach you how to beat him," he said. He was surprised when she squealed, talking over Simp's head at her brother.

"Oooh, you hear that, Chris? Deontae said he can teach me how to play Ping-Pong so I can beat you."

"More power to him," Chris said.

His lack of concern emboldened Simp. He pushed

his cap back off his forehead. "Three lessons and you can whip up on him." He got loud so his voice would carry Chris's way. "He a lightweight."

"I don't know about all that. I could end up being hopeless," Chrissy whispered, then bust out laughing. Simp couldn't help cracking a smile.

He stood up. "So what's up, son? Is it a bet?"

Chris took his time looking up from his conversation with Bean. Simp folded his arms to hide his clenched fist. He met Chris's bored gaze with a steely one.

"What bet?" Chris asked.

Simp channeled his coach's patience as he answered, "That I can teach your sister how to play good enough to beat you."

Chris shrugged. "What's in it for me?"

Rollie got in on it. "Okay, so if Chrissy lose, then Simp gotta let the girls teach him a dance he gotta do here at the rec in front of everybody." He put his hand up at Simp's look of disgust. "And if Chrissy win, Chris got wear one of her dance outfits next time we kicking it here at the rec. Like, for real chill in it while we hanging out."

"Man, how I'm gonna fit one of those things?" Chris scowled.

"Wait, a leotard or like a costume from a recital?" Tai asked, sitting up with interest.

Rollie shrugged. "I mean, either one gonna look crazy."

"He probably wouldn't fit one of her leotards," Bean volunteered, reasonably.

"I have a lot of outfits from recitals," Chrissy said. "I can hook him up."

"But you might try help him so he not embarrassed," Tai said. "Let somebody else pick one."

"He'll look ridiculous in any of them. I mean, I was a sunflower one time," Chrissy said, cracking the squad up. "Kind of hard to not be embarrassed in a yellow slip dress with 'sun rays' for sleeves."

"Oh, shoot, I vote that one," Mo said.

As the squad joked more about Chris in a tutu or dress, Simp's anger at Rollie for setting the stakes subsided. He couldn't dance—and only Rollie knew that—but he could teach Chrissy good enough for one round. He raised his voice, stopping all the chatter. "All right, whatever. I ain't gonna lose. It's a bet for me." He raised an eyebrow at Chris.

"It's dumb," Chris said, head shaking.

"It's just for fun," Chrissy said. "And remember, for real for real, I suck at Ping-Pong."

Chris sucked his teeth but stuck his hand out. "Whatever. Bet."

Simp slid his hand over Chris's and they gripped fingers.

Chrissy popped off the sofa. "You better start teaching me now."

"Ay, you only get three practices, remember?" Chris said.

"Yeah, yeah, I know," Simp said. The first twinge of uncertainty stung him. He turned to push Sheeda and Mo away from the table when he saw Coach Tez standing at the entrance of the rec room looking around. Champ pointed Simp's way. Coach Tez called for him with a single finger.

"I be back," Simp said.

A few heads turned as he walked across the room. Mostly dudes from the basketball team, probably wondering what was up. Simp wondered, too. His brain jumped from one thought to another, hoping he hadn't forgotten to do something, or worse, missed a call. His hand went to his belt loop and palmed the phone. He prayed to himself it hadn't buzzed while he was sitting there BSing with the squad.

He gave Coach Tez a pound and forced himself to

be casual. "What's up? You want me?"

Coach Tez put his arm around him. "Need talk to you for a taste." They walked slow, side by side as Coach Tez talked low. Simp lowered his head to hear better. "We got a little unfinished business."

Simp pulled his phone off his belt. "Did you call me?"

Coach Tez laughed. "Naw, little soldier. You good. I figured you would be here." His head turned as he watched a girl with leggings gripping her butt walk by. "Back in the day, this was the place to be on Tuesdays. Still is, I see. I see why with shorties walking around with everything out like that." He clapped his hand once. "But, naw, I got a little business. Let's hit the shed."

In a heartbeat his steps were long and fast. Simp kept up, but let Coach Tez lead. He automatically took a seat when they got inside. Coach Tez pulled up the other folding chair. Turning it backward, he straddled it and rested his arms on the chair's back. "You good?"

Confused, Simp answered cautiously. "Yeah?"

Coach Tez's laugh was loud in the cold, quiet shed. "That sounded like you asking me. You good?"

"Yeah," Simp said, confident but still confused. He jumped when the shed door opened with a creaky pop. His head swiveled around in time to see Angel, Coach

Tez's nephew, walk in. Relief flooded his heart. For a second he thought they were being ambushed. The image of him and Coach Tez getting shot up wavered in front of his eyes like a hazy illusion.

Angel sat on the edge of the desk, between their chairs. "My bad, Unc: I got held up. What up, Simp?" He put his fist out for a pound. Simp knocked it gently, then stuffed his hand into the pocket of his hoodie to hide the trembling.

"It's all right. We just got here," Coach Tez said. "I was telling Angel about your potential. You think you ready for a little more work?"

Simp looked from uncle to nephew. With their matching light skin and black wavy hair, they could have been brothers. Angel's swag was on low, but it seemed like that only made people like him more—girls and dudes. He'd always been cool with Simp. Now it seemed like he had Angel's approval. He processed it all as he nodded, wide-eyed. "Yeah, man. Whatever you need me do."

Coach Tez grinned. The diamonds in his T flashed at Simp. "Good. I still want you out there working the front for me." He raised an eyebrow then nodded when Simp indicated he understood. "But I want you do a few things with Angel on the outside."

Simp's heart raced. On the outside. Only trusted soldiers got to do anything outside of the Cove. And as far as Simp knew, Angel worked alone. He blinked hard to focus on Coach Tez's words. "We gon' see how it work out. If it does, then we can look at letting somebody else take your place out front."

Simp frowned. "What about Rollie?"

"What about him?" Coach Tez shrugged.

"I mean, I'mma still work the front with him, for now, right?" Simp knew it probably sounded like he was saying he couldn't do it without Rollie. He held his breath, waiting on Coach Tez to light into him.

Coach Tez flicked his head Simp's way. "Told you he was loyal. Not trying leave the buddy he got put on with. That's what's up." He gave Simp a long look. "That's why I know I'm right about you." He scratched at his eyebrow like he was thinking.

Simp felt like kicking himself for questioning. Backtracking would only make it worse. He quietly sweated it out, not ready for Coach Tez's proposal.

"Naw, I ain't trying break y'all up." He stroked his chin and cocked his head to the right. "But ay, little shorty that was balling with y'all a few days ago. That's your brother, right?"

"Yeah, Coach," Simp said. His throat closed in on him so it came out a croak.

They weren't talking about 'Rauders anymore. Why was Coach asking about Dre?

He leaned back in the chair, not liking the glint in Coach Tez's eyes.

Coach Tez nodded at Angel. "When I tell you little man is bad, there ain't no lies in it." Simp robotically tapped Coach's outstretched fist. "Shoot, I think he as good as you already, Simp."

Simp eased at the basketball talk, too fast. No sooner had he answered, "Yeah. He want try out in April if he pass fifth grade," Coach was back to business.

"He look like he can take care of his self. These runs work out, he might could take your place on the fence." Mistaking Simp's openmouthed silence for confusion, he assured him. "Like I said, though, it's only a few special runs. Nothing permanent. You and Rollie can still hold it down, together, for now. All right?"

It was a question that didn't need an answer. He got up from the chair and walked back behind the desk, dismissing Simp.

Simp mumbled good-bye and stood out in the cold

trying to piece it together. Coach Tez wanted to put Dre on.

Dre had been asking about balling for the Marauders for a minute now. Simp had always told him not to worry about it till he passed fifth grade. Now it was almost here. But the last thing he wanted was to have his brothers in the game. At least not till he had his own crew and could watch out for 'em. And maybe not then.

He tried imagining Dre working a shift. Sitting out near the entrance fence. Whooping out a call if the cops rolled through. Nodding through people in cars that crept into the neighborhood who knew they had no business there but doing business there just the same. That was the game.

He wasn't ready to think about Dre doing all that. But Coach hadn't given him a choice.

By the time he got home, the weight of the game was heavy on his shouders. He decided Dre wasn't ready. He would have to prove to Coach Tez that he could handle the hustle on his own. Once Coach saw that, he wouldn't need Dre.

Naw, not yet, he thought.

ROLLIE

Rollie played the song over in his head. He kept getting stuck on the same part. The bridge was a complicated series of rolls that sounded like rain hitting a bunch of tin cans. *Pa pat a pat pa pat pa pat.* It was the best part of the song because the beat would drop and only the drums held it down. It had to flow just right. But every time he hit that part, his rhythm was off.

Was it *pa pat pa pat* or *pat pat pat pa pat*?

He cursed under his breath as he stomped down the hall. He ripped his locker door open. He knew he shouldn't have hung out with the squad at the rec the other day. That was two hours he could have been listening to the audition song. Two hours that he could have been tapping the beat out, teaching his feet and hands what to do. It was called muscle memory and that only came with practice.

It was too many distractions right now. School, basketball, church choir, the hustle, the squad. Everything bled together.

He stared into his locker, a dim hole with books stacked neatly on a shelf and a black cinch bag with his musty gym uniform on the bottom, and summoned the beat. But it wouldn't obey.

He clinched his teeth and closed his eyes, willing the beat to infect him like a sneaky virus. Lockers banged shut beside him and rattled open a few feet down. He listened to it until the noises became a song. Then his lids relaxed. He rode the hallway's sounds. Seconds later, it merged from banging lockers to the pat of the drumline from the audition song, playing clear as a radio.

Mr. B was teaching him how to read and write music so he could capture sounds instead of having to memorize them. Until then, he only had the beat playing faintly in his head.

His hand drummed the locker beside him while his foot tapped an invisible pedal. He kept time to the beat, working to lock it in. He didn't feel the people brushing by him as they moved on to class. It was all about the beat.

Pa pat pa pat. Pa pat pat pat. Pa pat pa pat.

Pa pat pa . . . The beat scattered as a voice beside him called out, "What up, Rollie?"

He cursed to himself, gritted his teeth, hoping against hope whoever it was would just keep it moving. Instead, he heard the clunk as the beat killer leaned against the neighboring locker.

"Ay, yo, what's good?" it asked again.

The beat retreated like a girl jealous that he'd cut his eyes to watch another female pass by. He shut the locker door, defeated.

Zahveay Jenkins's face grinned up at him. "What you got in there, son?" He pretended to peer into the slits of Rollie's locker. "You ain't even hear me hollering at you. Must be some good stuff."

Nobody, except maybe Chris, really understood it when he started zoning. Getting mad at them for disrupting was pointless. He let it go and became a reluctant participant in the conversation. "Nah, I couldn't remember if today was a A or B day. Trying figure out which books to snatch up."

"Son, I did that last Tuesday and had to pay five dollars to rent a gym uniform." Zahveay's eyes rolled. He walked alongside Rollie, nearly arm to arm in the crowd's swell. They kept pace with the rest of the herd. "They be scamming you for real. Five dollars," he repeated, like the memory still hurt his pocket. "Ay, so you still with the 'Rauders right?" His words flowed right over Rollie's blank-faced nod like he already knew the answer. "Righ. Righ. I told Marcus you was. He said he thought you quit. I was like, naw, son, Rollie gon' ball till he make it." He imitated a jump shot.

Rollie wouldn't match Zahveay's smile. He hated rumors. No matter how small, trouble always followed 'em. What got to him was how even keeping to himself didn't stop people from assuming, guessing, or straight-up making things up. He infused his voice with steely annoyance. "People need step to the source if they want know. What Marcus asking for?" He glanced out of the corner of his eye at Zahveay, sizing him up.

"Ay, yo, don't take it wrong." Zahveay held up his hands in surrender. "You know the Pumas always scoping out the competition. No shade, but I ain't got no piece of it either way. Ioun live in the Cove no more but I ain't Del Rio Crossings homegrown." There was bitterness in his laugh. "So, there it is. Guess he asked me 'cause he knew me and you was cool."

Rollie stopped dead in the middle of the hallway. The flow behind them stuttered, then peeled around. "Yeah, well, let whoever want know, I'm still down with the 'Rauders. Feeling that?"

Zahveay's face tensed. "It ain't like that, man." His shoulders straightened as he spat, "I ain't no messenger boy."

Rollie wanted to point out that he kind of was. He left it alone.

Zahveay had always been that dude that buzzed around like a gnat determined to land on you no matter how much you swatted. When he lived in the Cove he'd flitted in and out, never down with any one set. Rollie didn't see him as a friend, but he didn't have nothing against him, either. Then he'd moved to Del Rio Crossings back in sixth grade. There wasn't no way Zah was tight with Marcus and 'nem after only two years in the Crossings. It didn't work that way around there. Still, his question felt like somebody poking a hive with a big stick to see if bees still lived there.

Rollie didn't like it, but he played along. "Marcus already know what kind of whupping in store for him at the J. Martins. He just need be ready for the spanking."

Zahveay laughed, then took a quick look over his shoulder before lowering his voice. "I hear that. Low-key, you know I'm with the 'Rauders from day one." His eyebrow cocked high. "But you gotta get in where you fit in. I live in the Crossings now. So . . ." He trailed off then quickly added, "I don't have beef with nobody. It's swazy."

Rollie doubted Zah would ever fit in over in the Crossings. People there had an uneasy and fragile relationship with the Cove, made shakier by feuding basketball teams and wannabe hustlers always trying to claim territory. Zah was right—he didn't really belong anywhere anymore. But that was Zah's business. He blinked back any sympathy. "Righ. Do what you got to."

"All day. Later, son," Zahveay said, his hand out for a pound.

Rollie barely tapped back, then watched as Zah blended into the crowd. Next thing he knew Simp was beside him, snarling, "Was that Zahvee? What he want?" He cupped his hand making a C. "All about that Cove, boy," he hollered at the dot that had been Zah seconds before.

"Snooping for the Pumas," Rollie said, not bothering to correct Simp on pronouncing the dude's name. Simp had never liked Zahveay. Calling him out his name was the level of disrespect he probably wanted to show. He sliced through the crowd to their classroom, Simp on his heels, questioning.

"Zahvee hooping with the Pumas now? That fool can't ball." His frown wrinkled deeper at Rollie's shrug. "What did he think you was gon' tell him?"

"He asked was I still playing, that's all," Rollie said, hoping Simp would pick up on how much he didn't care.

Simp only got more hyped. His desk skittered several inches as he slammed himself into the seat. "Why he want know? And hell yeah, you still playing." His eyes shot to the front of the room, checking for the teacher before going on. "Why would anybody wonder if you on the team? What? They questioning if you still down with 'Rauders?"

With Simp everything was about being with or against somebody. Either you were for the Cove or against it. With the 'Rauders or against them. On Tez's team or not. Rollie slid into the desk beside Simp and tried to look bored. "Son, it's Zahveay." He put his hands up like *c'mon*. "You know Zah always looking for somebody to be down with."

Simp's eyes questioned, wanting more answers than Rollie had time or desire to give. The wrinkle in his brow eased, then appeared again as he thought it over. Finally, he sucked his teeth. "I ain't never like dude no way. Now he over at Del Rio Crossings probably telling whatever he know about 'Rauders."

Rollie chuckled. "That ain't much since he wasn't on the team."

"That probably ain't gon' stop him from jawing," Simp said.

"I told him tell Marcus get ready for dat spanking," Rollie said.

Simp cackled loud. "I know that's right. Run tell dat," he hollered out to the air. "Don't be trusting that punk. Look at him, low-key messenger boy." He snorted in disgust.

Their tech ed teacher's demand for quiet forced an end to the conversation. Time to build something.

Rollie let the encounter go and was ready to politely pay attention to Ms. Pumphrey's take on how to use a T square, until the demo beat slithered into his ear. *Pa pat pat.* And just like that, it was back spreading into his brain forcing his fingers to tap. Rollie gave into it, schoolwork forgotten.

By the end of the day, the beat was finally ingrained in his head. He had to practice it. The thought of that night's basketball practice was a breezy whisper. Maybe he could make it. Maybe he couldn't.

The beat. He had to practice the beat. His legs couldn't move fast enough to meet Mr. B in the studio.

Rollie stood inches shy of the narrow window cut into the door and listened to the music floating from behind the studio door. He hated when people stuck their faces in it and gawked. He'd definitely peeked into the dance rooms before, but it made sense to watch dance. People didn't need to peek into the music studios to hear what was going on.

From behind the door, the beat crested, rolled, then hit another peak. Somebody was going H.A.M. on the drums. He shifted so one eye could see through the window. Mr. B's black power fist bobbed furiously in his thick afro as his head nodded to each drum crash. In contrast, his hands moved smoothly, tapping each beat.

Lost in it, Rollie leaned into the door. It swayed open. He considered running away but the movement had caught Mr. B's attention. "Come on in," he said.

"My bad. I didn't mean to interrupt you," Rollie

said. He took a baby step inside. "If you busy, I just see you tomorrow during TAG."

Mr. B cuffed the drumsticks on his lap. "Nope. You got it. What's on your mind?"

"My mother gave me permission to audition for TRB."

"Yes, she did." Mr. B laughed. "It took me a good hour to read through her whole e-mail of questions."

Rollie's face blazed. "Yeah. I mean, it's more my grandmother than her. She still not sure it's legit."

Mr. B nodded, unbothered.

Rollie took a seat in front of the drums. The room was dim except two lights above the drum set. He loved it here. He belonged here. He didn't want to leave.

"I was hoping I could practice the audition song," Rollie said. He shrunk and prayed Mr. B said yes. He'd already missed the bus. And still didn't know how he was getting home.

"Good idea. Your mother know you staying after?" Mr. B asked. He slid effortlessly from behind the drums. "I think question number five was, could I send her the days you'd be rehearsing."

Rollie rolled his eyes. That was definitely G-ma's question. Just trying make sure he didn't miss choir.

"Having protective parents isn't the worst thing in

the world," Mr. B said. "Not even close to the worst."

"I guess. But no, they don't know I'm here. I'm supposed to be at basketball practice, for real," Rollie said with a sigh. "But I need to get this beat outta my head. I mean, not out of my head because I need it in my head. But I need to practice. I—"

"I understand." Mr. B flicked his head at the drums. "Go on. Get in a warm-up. Then I'll tape you and we can go over what needs work."

Rollie was up and behind the drums in seconds. As soon as he sat down, his phone buzzed hard, four times in a row.

"Why don't you check that. In case it's your mom or grandmom," Mr. B said. "That'll give me time to set up to record."

"My grandmother don't text," Rollie said, the laugh dying in his throat as he saw the text from Simp.

GreatEight: *Where u at? U miss da bus?*

Couldn't Simp be off him for just a minute?

He didn't know how to answer. If he said yes, Simp would just tell Tez and they'd send one of the older players to scoop him up. If he said no . . .

Rollie didn't know what would happen. The J. Martins was Saturday. Plus, Tez was probably announcing the starting five tonight. He should be there. Somebody could still pick him up in time for practice if he said he missed the bus. That would give him at least twenty minutes to rehearse.

He needed more than that, though.

He texted his mother: *Stayed after school to rehearse. Mr. B gonna drop me home.*

After, he stared at his phone, still unsure.

Another message buzzed in.

GreatEight: *u need somebody come get u??????* 😛

"Everything all right?" Mr. B asked, suddenly beside him.

"Ay, um . . . can you take me home?" Rollie added quickly, "I wanted to get the beat down so bad I wasn't thinking how I was gonna get home. If you can't—"

Mr. B reassured him. "The beat gets you like that sometimes. If it's okay with your mother, yes."

"Thanks," Rollie said.

He rubbed the phone like it was a magic lamp that would give him three wishes or at least the answer for Simp. But no genie came out, and if there was a right answer it was deeper than he felt like digging. He put the phone on silent. As if Simp sensed his avoidance, the phone lit up with another message.

GreatEight: *Man ur ass better be hurt or dead. dayum*

Yeah, I know, Rollie thought bitterly. He dropped the phone onto his backpack.

"Whatever it is, play through it," Mr. B said. He sat down in the front row, audience of one. "A bad grade. A teacher that got on your nerves. Friends acting up. Whatever it is. Beat it out of those drums. Let's go."

Rollie knew he would still have to deal with all of it later. Either tonight. On the bus in the morning. At practice tomorrow. Whenever. The madness would still be there. It always was. Still, the advice soothed his frayed nerves.

He closed his eyes. Raised the sticks. Exhaled and went off.

SIMP

The "other" side of Del Rio Bay came into focus as the car cruised across the bridge. Trees, trees, and more trees. The Cove was surrounded by trees. It was hidden from the main road because of them, a hood always alive with people up and down the street, streaming from their houses to the rec or the courts or cutting through the woods to hit the Wa. These trees opened up to huge mansions sitting high on the hill above the bay's dirty green water. One had a pool right on the edge. Another had a tennis court. Their windows were big eyes watching them cross. Simp stared back and wondered out loud, "Are those hotels?"

There was no cruelty in Angel's laugh as he craned his neck to catch what Simp was gaping at, before it went out of view.

"Naw, they just houses. Crazy huh?"

Crazy for sure. At least four Cove row houses could fit inside any of the houses standing watch over the water. He couldn't imagine only one family living inside, but one thing he knew—you had to make mad dough to buy a house like that.

He was all about that. That's why he was here, making a run with Angel.

Bolts of lightning cracked in his belly. His knee jiggled to keep the electricity from coursing through him and out of his mouth in the form of stupid questions like: Where were they going? What did Angel want him to do? Wasn't Angel worried the police might be clocking him?

He looked in the side mirror, half expecting to see leecee's blue and red police lights behind them.

Being out of the Cove made him nervous. His ears were tuned to the low-pitched whistle that meant cops was coming through. He knew the shortcuts and places to disappear before they rounded the corner where him and Rollie stood watch. At home, he never worried about getting caught.

Now he felt naked. Even in the car, he wanted to duck down. He reached to pull up his hoodie, but it wasn't there. Angel had told him not to wear one. No explanation, just told him no hats, no hoodies.

Simp rubbed absently at his locs, feeling even more exposed.

"Everything good?" Angel asked.

"Yeah. I'm swazy," Simp said, forcing himself upright.

"Ay, yo, relax. Ain't gonna be a quiz or anything," Angel said. He turned the radio up, sang a few bars of the song then talked above the music. "Captains be named soon, right?"

Simp rubbed his hands together. "Yeah. Why, you know something?"

"Nah. Shoot, if I did I wouldn't say nothing. You know how my uncle is with that team." Angel's head shook side to side. "Y'all like his kids or something. But—" His eyebrow rose. "If you was made captain, you ready for all the honeys 'bout to jock you, though?"

A grin broke across Simp's face.

Simp tapped Angel's outstretched fist with his own, then snatched it back as he thought about Tez's feelings about girlfriends. "Coach want us focus on the game, for real."

Angel snorted. "Whatever. I love my uncle, but if I gotta choose between balling and a shorty, no contest the shorty gets the dub."

Simp didn't have to worry about that choice. Couldn't imagine having that problem. But it felt good talking to Angel about that kind of stuff. He relaxed as Angel went on about some girl he was hollering at. She lived somewhere on this side of Del Rio Bay and sounded rich. Simp wanted to ask Angel so bad did she know he was a dough boy. He wouldn't have ever actually asked—it wasn't none of his business—and Angel pulled up to a gas station, killing the chance.

There were two other cars at the pump.

Angel pulled his Civic on to the other side of the pump. He walked toward the pay window and saw somebody he knew. As the two of them went in for a pound, Simp looked down at his phone. He had a message from Chrissy: *lesson today?*

He hit her back: *can't. tomorrow?*

Chriss-E: *ok* 😬

The emoji stared back at him. Big, yellow, and grinning. Chrissy was vibing with him and he wasn't even captain (yet)—maybe Angel was right. He was reconsidering—maybe they'd be back in time for him to kick it with Chrissy today—when the car door opened with a blast of cold air.

Angel rubbed his hands together and blew on them. "You good?" His eyes quizzed Simp.

Still thinking about the text, Simp answered happily, "Yeah." More than good, he thought.

"One more stop. You want a soda or chips or something?" Angel asked.

"Naw, I'm all right," Simp said, thinking: One more stop? Where had the first one been?

Angel pulled into a convenience store and ran in. Simp looked around, confused, waiting for something to happen. There were half a dozen cars at the convenience store. One of the workers stood outside, smoking a cigarette. Two girls, one White, one Black, were sitting on the curb at the store's edge. He leaned his head back on the seat, pretending to be sleeping but kept his eyes on the two girls. They had to be Angel's customers.

A flash of movement to his left caught his eye. He jerked his head up.

Angel was laughing at something a dude that was

going inside the store said. They chopped it up a few more seconds, then gripped. In seconds him and the orange soda he carried were back in the car.

When they were on the bridge, heading home, Angel cracked open the soda. He took a swig, then said, "And that's it."

He chugged the soda and belched loud as Simp trudged through the information racing in his mind. This was the special run? Angel needed gas and a cold, cold beverage?

He must have missed something. He went over everything he'd seen and came up blank. Finally, he gave up.

"What you mean?" he asked.

Angel scowled at him. "Wasn't you watching?"

"I mean, I was," Simp sputtered. He thought harder, this time out loud. "I saw you speak to that dude at the C-store."

"That's all you saw?" Angel asked.

His eyebrows were knitted like he was ready go off 'cause Simp was failing a test he hadn't known he was taking. Except he had known this was a test. Why hadn't he paid more attention? Before Simp could fall over himself explaining, Angel bust out laughing.

"Cool. Cool. That mean I still got that touch then."

Simp was relieved and ashamed. He soaked it all in as Angel explained.

"You never saw me hand off anything?" Angel quizzed.

Simp shook his head, afraid he'd sound stupid if said anything more.

"You didn't see them hand me nothing?" Angel nodded in approval at Simp's denial. "That's the game. You see what I want you to see."

"So that's what happened at the C-store?" Simp asked, connecting Angel's words with the pictures in his memory.

"And the gas station," Angel said. He turned the radio down. "You was watching, right?"

"Yeah, I saw you talk to that White dude," Simp said, instantly guilty for texting Chrissy. He had seen it; he just didn't realize what he was seeing.

This was the game, the real game. He had to pay attention. To everything. To anything. He wanted to beg Angel to take him out again, but knew he had to wait on the invitation. If it came, he'd show Angel he had what it took.

Then he remembered Coach Tez talking about replacing

him, in the front, with Dre. And for the first time, he wasn't sure if he wanted the invitation to come or not.

He was excited for the run, but not if it meant Dre getting put on. He had been wanting to talk to Rollie about it first. See what he thought and maybe see if Rollie had some ideas on what he should do. But Rollie was ghost lately. When they did see each other, it was mainly in practice. They knew better than to talk then. And he couldn't text him about it. Rule number two of the game: Don't let your phone get you caught up.

He was gonna have to handle this his self.

He used his lesson with Chrissy to keep it all off his mind. It definitely wasn't a bad way to pass time.

"Like this?" Chrissy asked. She raised the Ping-Pong ball to her nose, dropped it to the table, then swatted it, hard, with the paddle. The ball landed on her side of the table, bounced once, then skittered wildly across the floor. "Sorry, Deontae."

Simp chased after it, torn between laughing and being mad. Chrissy wasn't getting any better. He wasn't about to get clowned in front of everybody because she couldn't control a tiny ball.

"Yo, y'all almost done?" Squirt asked. "How long ol' girl gon' keep you chasing that ball?"

"Don't worry 'bout it, punk," Simp said, snatching the ball from Squirt.

He swallowed his frustration. Chrissy was cool. And he liked the way his name sounded coming from her mouth. She didn't say it all hard like some people, always emphasizing each syllable like it was three separate names: Dee-On-Tay. With Chrissy it was Deon-tay. He couldn't stay mad with her.

"Don't take this wrong, but I think you forget how tall you are," he said when he returned to the table. "Don't serve the ball so high." He brought his hand a few inches above the table, tossed it lightly into the air, then sent it flying gently her way. "Tap it back," he instructed, pleased when she did.

They volleyed longer than they had in their first practice until he smacked the ball hard enough for her to flinch and miss.

"How come that never works when I try it?" she said, laughing.

"I got that touch," he said, with a wink. "For real, though, it's about da flick of dat wrist."

Chrissy's shoulders bounced and dipped to her own

beat as she sang, "He got da flick of dat wrist. Da flick of dat wrist."

He admired her moves. "I be forgetting you a dancer."

"You mean you forget I do more than ballet?" She raised an eyebrow at him.

"True, true." Simp threw his paddle at Squirt. "Your game." He threw a middle finger as Squirt cussed him out and plopped onto the sofa farthest from the Ping-Pong table.

"You done with me already?" Chrissy sat down beside him. She fanned at herself.

"We been at it for, like, thirty minutes," he said, knowing he'd stay another two hours if it meant standing behind her to help her serve.

"But we only allowed one more lesson and I still suck." She touched his arm. "I mean, that's not your fault, though. You trying."

"For real, if you just stop serving so high I think you halfway there."

Chrissy sat back with a soft thud. "Maybe. Don't underestimate how badly my brother don't want to wear that sunflower costume."

"You be good. Like you said, we got one more lesson."

There was a tug on his locs. It sent a tingle down

his neck. "How long you been growing these?" Chrissy asked.

His tongue struggled to form the words right. He cleared his throat. "Since fifth grade."

"Dang." Chrissy pulled gently, stretching the loc until it reached the bottom of his neck. "They're so long. Who be tightening 'em up for you?"

"Broad up in first court," he said.

Chrissy laughed. "Broad. So, like, no name or anything?" Her head whipped to look down at her phone. "It's Mila. Her and the girls ready to head this way."

"Shoot. It's five thirty already?" he asked, patting his pocket for his phone. "My bad. I gotta dip."

He was half way to the door when she called out, "Same time next week?"

"Yeah. I got you." He started to head out. He couldn't be late to practice, not today. Then he strode over to her. "Ay, 'Rauders got a tourney on Saturday. You should come. Tai and Bean know where it be."

Simp wasn't sure, but it looked like Chrissy's smile got bigger. And did he hear her say "Okay" real quiet? He turned heel and jogged toward the gym, letting each pound on the ground squash down the warm joy creeping into his heart. No time for shorties right now, he told himself. Captains were being named today.

Him and Rollie used to talk about being co-captains all the time. Now Rollie wasn't even gonna start Saturday's game. Remembering Coach Tez's pursed lips as he scanned the gym looking for Rollie the other day pierced Simp. If he'd asked him where Rollie was, Simp had been prepared to lie and say Rollie had missed the bus. He'd been a little ashamed at how relieved he was when Coach Tez hadn't bothered to ask.

Rollie had known better than to miss the practice where starting five was announced. It was Coach Tez's way of making sure they knew nobody was guaranteed to start every week.

Luckily, they had a deep team. Practically anybody could start and still give fools a run because being second-string 'Rauders meant you was good, just not great. But this would be the first time Rollie hadn't started since they joined the team. No way Coach Tez would pick him to be a captain now.

Everything was so crazy.

Simp slowed down right before he entered the gym and sauntered in like there was never a doubt he'd be on time. He inhaled deep through his nose and let it trickle out to slow his racing heart. He dapped up and gave pounds on his way to drop his bag on the sideline.

He couldn't hold his grin back when Rollie came in, on time, beating Coach Tez for once.

"Punk, I was ready curb your ass if you ain't show up today," Simp said. The joy in his heart tripled when Rollie smiled, a real smile, and teased back.

"How you gonna curb the best point guard 'Rauders seen since Stimpy Stevens?" Rollie said, pretending to juke then fade into a jump shot.

They gripped fingers, then started undressing. Players milled around them, taking their time getting warm-ups off and stretching. Simp dropped to the floor, spread his legs, and eased into a hamstring stretch. Rollie did the same across from him and put his arms out. Simp grabbed at his elbows and helped pull Rollie into a stretch.

"Maybe Coach Tez will change his mind and let you start on Saturday," he said, raising his voice loud enough over the team's trash talking.

"I'm good. Rules are rules, right?" Rollie said, pulling Simp toward him in the stretch.

"He probably sub you in quick, though," Simp said, hopeful.

"It's whatever," Rollie said.

Simp stayed in the stretch a second longer to process what he was hearing. When he came up, he let go of Rollie's arm and looked around. No one was paying attention. Champ threw a ball at J-Roach's head. They started shadowboxing, everybody else egging them on.

The few minutes before Coach Tez showed up were the easiest part of practice. Nobody ever said it out loud, but it was also their favorite part. The only time nobody was worried about getting punished for not hustling enough or being yelled at for missing a shot.

Even Simp liked those few minutes of peace before the big general showed up.

"Son, for real, you better start caring." He put his hands up at Rollie's frown. "No shade. Do you. But when you step on the court, you got be all the way down. Know what I'm sayin'?"

"I'm here, ain't I?" Rollie said.

"Barely," Simp snapped back.

"Just be off me. You acting like my grandmoms, for real, for real," Rollie said. He put his legs together and put his nose down to his knees.

Simp wasn't that flexible. He imitated the move and hovered above his knees. He hissed in Rollie's direction.

"Punk, I'm the only one standing between you and Coach booting you off the team. You should be grateful."

"Oh, my bad. Forgot you was the one that got us all hooked up with Tez." Rollie straightened up and saluted. "Thanks for that, partner."

Simp's thoughts were moving too fast. His brain couldn't grab on to which thing to respond to first. Rollie didn't give him the chance.

"Look, you can stop feeling like you need to babysit me. Whether I'm on the team or not between me and Tez."

He went to stand. Out of reflex Simp gripped his arm.

"Wait, hold up."

He hated how grateful he felt that Rollie stayed seated. Simp crossed one leg over the other and the stupid warm gratefulness spread when Rollie followed along.

"I ain't mean come off like that," Simp said. His words sped up like a shot clock was over his head. "But, son, Coach making moves. Real moves." At Rollie's confused scowl he whispered, "He sent me on a run with Angel last week."

Rollie's wide-eyed surprise was the reaction he'd hoped for. Somewhere in there Rollie still cared.

"He got you running outside the hood?" Rollie whispered.

Simp nodded. "I wanted to tell you but . . . I mean, you ain't been around a lot."

He really had wanted to tell Rollie, but there was also a part of him that had liked the secrecy of the run. Liked that Coach Tez trusted him enough to send him on his own. But Rollie's shoulders seemed to sag as he answered, "It's all right," and Simp couldn't help reassuring him.

"He still down for keeping me and you together." He parroted their coach's words: "It's just a few special runs."

Rollie's eyes darted to the doorway. His lips were parted to speak but no words came out. It made Simp want to tell him everything—about how the run worked and about Coach Tez talking about putting Dre on. Before he could say anything, a whistle shrieked. Tez strode across the floor. "Ay, everybody gather 'round and congratulate your new captain."

Everyone seemed to freeze then, on cue, fell into a small crowd behind their coach as he walked.

Simp scrambled up, unsure where to walk. Was Tez coming toward him?

The only other player behind Simp was Cappy, racing to recover a stray ball. Simp stepped aside to fall in line with his teammates when Tez stopped in front of him.

"Shouldn't nobody be surprised. Nobody work harder than this dude, right here," Tez said. He pulled a whistle dangling from a thick silver chain from his pocket. He put it around Simp's neck. "From day one he been my floor general. He follow orders like a good soldier but also know how to command respect on the floor. Keep putting in that work, Deontae."

Simp let himself be pulled into Tez's pound and hug. His teammates clapped it up around them. Slapping his back and congratulating him. He'd made it. No matter what happened after this he would forever be a 'Rauder captain.

Everybody knew that meant he was a trusted soldier repping his team and his hood. 'Rauders All Day.

The sting of tears horrified him. He dipped his head, pretending to adjust the band keeping his locs in place.

Tez's laugh boomed through the gym. "All right, oun want this little knucklehead think he got give a speech or something." He slapped Simp on the back. "Start your practice, Captain."

Simp blew the whistle, hard. "Jump drill," he said, shouting to purge the welling emotion.

Players scattered and took their place on the court. Rollie whispered his congratulations and gripped Simp's shoulder as he walked by.

Beaming, Coach Tez gestured to the floor. "They all yours."

Simp tucked the whistle into his shirt and joined his teammates.

He was captain now. Team first. Hustle hard—on the court and off.

No matter what it took.

ROLLIE

Rollie didn't lie a lot. Not with his mouth, anyway. Telling lies always came back on him. Like the time him and Simp had stole a game cartridge from the rec center. They were going to bring it back at the next Open Play night, but Mack, the rec director, had noticed it was missing and alerted the neighborhood.

Rollie had swore to G-ma he had no idea where the game was. She'd gone off about how kids didn't know no better than to steal from what little they had in their own neighborhood. And by then it was too late to get it back unnoticed.

Since everybody had to sign in to Open Play nights,

all Mack had to do was grill everybody on the list. Nobody was about to catch a case for something they didn't do. Simp had lied smoothly, confident they'd be able to drop the game in the lobby and pretend they'd found it. But Rollie had caved under the pressure. He ended up confessing to Mack and getting suspended from Open Play for a month. Which wasn't nothing. G-ma wouldn't let him hang out at the rec for the entire summer, as punishment.

He'd been eight. After that, he kept outright lying to a minimum. The problem was, he'd gotten better at quiet lying. Not saying anything was the same as lying, but sometimes it couldn't be helped.

Sitting in the gym at the J. Martins pretending he was as hyped as everybody else was a lie. But Rollie desperately wanted it not to be. He willed himself to pretend this was just one big indoor street ball game, so he'd get that electricity back.

All around him, Marauders huddled in different modes of stretch, some with headphones to help get their game face on, others talking loud over the noise of the crowd. The gymnasium was packed. When they'd arrived early that morning, to watch the little boys, the crowd was mainly handfuls of parents and younger siblings who still looked like they had sleep in their eyes.

Rollie had watched the games, amused. The young boys were balling hard, fouling more than they needed to establish who was boss with the rock. Now most of them and their parents remained in the stands to watch the Marauders play the Pumas.

His mother sat with her best friend, Ms. Taylor, just far enough from the official parents' section to avoid the nonsense. The parents always got too rowdy for her. Yet she was close enough to blend in with her black-and-gold Marauders spirit T.

Simp's mother, Ms. Niqa, was also there with his brothers. They were already up and down running from the bleachers to the concession stand. Rollie couldn't understand how she could possibly hear whoever she was talking to on the phone. All he knew was she probably wouldn't stay the whole game. She never did. Before she disappeared, she usually found a way to leave Simp's brothers with somebody.

Tai sat deep in conversation with Mila, Sheeda, Mo, and Chrissy at the top bleachers with a bunch of other kids from Pirates Cove.

Half the neighborhood was there.

Of course. It was a big game. The winner of the J. Martins would get the number one seed and get an easy schedule leading to the 'Peake. As long as the 'Rauders were good, the Cove always turned out. And the 'Rauders were always good. The hood love pulsated throughout the gym.

Never to be outdone, Del Rio Crossings fans, blinding in their silver-and-white gear, took up the visitors' side of the gym. Rollie's eyes strayed to a group of girls who had designated themselves the official cheerleaders. They insisted on making up new chants every few minutes. When the crowd joined in, they got louder. When the crowd wasn't feeling the new chant and grew quiet, the girls rolled their eyes and purposely kept the chant going on longer.

The energy in the room was a furious ball of noise and movement. Tez let Simp handle warm-ups while he paced the sidelines taking care of "business" with Coach Monty and people at the score table. It was a circus, in a good way. Rollie laid back in a stretch and closed his eyes, preparing himself to work.

Before things got complicated, he had loved sweating and pushing his body up and down the court for the 'Rauders. Loved the drills and even the contact when it got rough. Loved that his body was so tired after games that when he went to bed his mind was empty enough to hear the beats and melodies playing deep inside him.

He needed that more than ever, right now. As long as he was on the 'Rauders, he needed it to help his music.

As he melted into his stretch, the sounds became pulsing beats behind his lids.

Simp barked, "Two more minutes stretching then hit the shootaround." His voice came from above Rollie's head. "Need me stretch out your hammies?"

In answer, Rollie lifted his right leg. Simp towered above him, pressing the leg back gently. "Ready get at 'em?"

"That's word. It's mad energy in here," Rollie said. "I didn't know Tai and 'nem was coming."

"Everybody know what's up. They 'bout to get a show." Simp's eyes narrowed. "I see punk-ass Marcus the captain this year."

"Hmph," Rollie said, focused on breathing so his leg wouldn't tense.

Simp's eyes stayed fixed across the room. "Ay, yo, why you think Marcus think you wasn't on the team no more?"

He had no idea what Simp was talking about, then his conversation with Zahveay flashed—a memory based more on his audition beat than whatever Zah had been talking about. "It probably ain't nothing. He just digging," Rollie said.

"I mean, let's say it's just smack, like you said earlier—" Simp's face hovered from above as he continued, "Why Marcus send a messenger?"

"Even if Marcus asked him about me, it didn't mean he told Zah to come ask me," Rollie said. "Yo, Zah probably like a little girl with a secret. Now he got a reason to say something to Marcus. Marcus probably be, like, man, what you telling me for?"

He laughed at the vision, glad when Simp laughed along. Simp let his leg down and Rollie thrust the other in the air, letting it be pressed until the muscle put up a stop sign.

"You probably right. But, I'm saying, everybody that grin in your face ain't your boy," Simp said. He leaned in with more pressure. "Even if you was cool with yo when he lived here, he in Crossings territory now. You can't be trusting everybody. Let him ride."

"You know how it get before the 'Peake," Rollie said, wanting to squash the whole thing. "Everybody be talking much smack. You letting 'em get in your head."

"Never that," Simp said defensively before grinning, his fist outstretched. "But if he want know if you still down, let's show him."

They bumped fists.

At the blow of the ref's whistle, the hunger for basketball in Rollie awakened. He put on the face and swag for the role. Nothing else existed as he ran up and down the court, hustling for every point.

Sweat stung his eyes. The crowds roar rang in his ears.

The refs stopped the game twice—once when Coach Tez stepped onto the court complaining about a call and then when a Pumas fan chugged water at a ref for calling a technical foul. Each time, the ref warned that the coaches and fans were out of pocket and would ruin it for the players if they kept it up.

It was a nice speech, wasted on the heated crowd. The noise drowned out the ref's whistle, and confusion on the floor led to shoving and complaints to the ref that he was missing calls. Number one ranking was at stake— everybody in the gym had the game under a microscope so whoever lost could claim they were robbed.

It was crazy and Rollie loved it. Games were the

only time it was about basketball.

He and Simp controlled the pace for the 'Rauders.

Rollie strolled down the court then sped past his defender, passing the ball to Simp who dominated the middle, always prepared to nestle the ball into the net. But the Pumas were ready. The entire game went basket for basket, foul for foul. With thirty seconds left the game was tied.

Coach Tez called a play they'd perfected.

Rollie tossed the ball to J-Roach. The dude defending him, predicting that J-Roach and Rollie would pass it back and forth until they had to shoot, played him hard. There was just enough space between them so dude could claim (barely) he wasn't touching.

Rollie edged toward him, backing him up. Testing the dude's willingness to foul him. Rollie was good on the free throw line. He dribbled, eating up as much time as he could. If they scored, he didn't want to leave any time for the Pumas to tie it back up.

He put his shoulder down, daring to get closer to his defender. If dude was going to foul Rollie, he had to decide now. Either he was going to risk Rollie taking and making a shot or being responsible for Rollie getting on the free throw line to take two. Knowing this, Rollie leaned in, nearly touching dude's stomach, and the guy threw his hands up and swayed back just enough for Rollie to pull up, pretend to shoot, and pass the ball to Simp.

It took only seconds, but it was enough time for Rollie to see Simp catch the ball out of the air and smash it into the basket. The buzzer, mean and final, signaled the game's end.

Rollie yelped in victory and ran to Simp. The team huddled around them celebrating. A few Pumas got stuck in the middle and began elbowing their way out.

"Watch out, punk," Simp said as Marcus angled his elbow at Cappy.

"You watch out, mark," Marcus said, chin up and ready for the fight.

Rollie placed his hand on Simp's chest to back him up, as much as he could in the middle of the sweaty bodies. They didn't need to fight. The refs were known to note it and penalize the teams the next time they played.

It was too late. Rollie was slammed into Simp as more bodies piled out of the stands and onto the floor.

"Yeah, we see y'all at the 'Peake," a Puma fan,

somebody's uncle or father, snarled in Simp's face.

"And what?" Simp said, bucking up.

Rollie shifted, rocking on his feet, as they got pushed and shoved. Puma fans yapped at players. 'Rauder fans yapped back. Players pushed to get space. He couldn't see beyond the few people closing him in. Marcus and Simp were still in each other's faces, Rollie stuck halfway between them.

"You ain't nothing, son. Step to me outside this gym," Marcus said.

"Yeah, all right," Simp said. "And I'mma bring my knot with me, help you buy some new kicks instead of those raggedy-ass J's you always rockin'."

Marcus went headfirst toward Simp, knocking Rollie out of the way.

Cappy grabbed Marcus's jersey. When Rollie got his footing, the entire team was either pulling a Puma off another teammate or going at one of them. He stood, the high from the game fading and tainted, unsure what to do.

Tez stepped into the fray and shook Cappy and Marcus apart. Within seconds, Pumas' coach West was beside his player. For a second he looked like he wasn't sure whether he wanted to help Marcus fight or break it up. When he saw Tez easing Simp back, he did the same with his captain.

Tez slowly walked his players back from the ruckus, raising an eyebrow, touching an arm until they got the message and followed.

The refs, their job done, stood off to the side disapproving. A 'Rauders/Pumas game was exciting, but nobody liked the drama that was part of the package. Eventually, the fans exhausted their bravado. With the tension lifting, Rollie's joy returned.

He dapped Simp up. "Number one, son."

Simp grinned. "That's word." He nodded at Marcus in the middle of the court getting a hushed talk from his coach. "He can go home mad if he want. Either way, he going home number two."

He and Simp laughed. On cue Marcus looked over, glaring.

Simp gave him the finger and laughed louder.

Rollie rode off the high for days. He'd be sitting in class and suddenly his body would swell, remembering the wave of the crowd's love, of his team's excitement as they rushed Simp after the game. It nourished him and got the juices of his brain flowing. He kept beat to the 'nome so well in his TAG session, Mr. B had wondered if he'd been sneaking into the music room to practice at night.

He wanted to ride the wave forever or at least until his audition.

He threw his gold practice jersey on and smoothed his hair down with a brush. The waves were thick and bushy. Not really long except to his grandmother, who considered anything not freshly cut down to a caesar too long.

Weekly trips to the barbershop were right up there with going to church, to G-ma.

"Unah, don't be trying to grow those plaits. Be out here looking crazy with those things bushing out your scalp like you a shrub gone wild," she'd argued when he'd skipped two weeks in a row.

"They locs, not plaits, G-ma. And I'm just trying to get a little fade," he'd said.

But she'd been insistent and made sure he was at the barbershop the next day.

Little stupid stuff like that was a signal to his grandmother that the streets were claiming him. It made what he did for Tez even worse because he was sure if she ever found out, it would give her a heart attack. Not one of those fake "you disappointed me" kind, either. He was convinced she'd keel over from the hurt and embarrassment of him being a hustler.

All the more reason he worked to hide it.

He rubbed some cream in his hands and ran them down his scalp. The hair was only a few days overdue for a cut, but it curled from the cream's moisture. His brown eyes were wide apart, his nose a small bump in the middle of the space. He stared at himself, in the mirror, looking for signs that the streets had claimed him. He looked like he always did. It was on the inside where he felt different.

And he wasn't sure what to do about it.

Simp's voice came from downstairs.

Rollie couldn't remember the last time he had stopped by so they could walk to practice together. He grabbed his duffel and galloped down the stairs, joining the small circle.

His mother was letting Simp out of a hug. She took a step back, arms folded, ready to get into a conversation. "How you been, Deontae? You staying out of trouble?"

She didn't mean anything by the question. It was just his mother being . . . a mother. That didn't stop Simp from looking at Rollie like he was wondering if Rollie had somehow been able to have a conversation about what Simp was doing in the streets without telling on himself. By the time Rollie shrugged his jacket on, the look was gone and all that was left was Simp smiling politely, his top lip mostly covering the platinum cap.

"Yes, ma'am. For real, oun have nobody to hang with since Rollie always be after school."

Rollie's mother's face, the female version of her son, lit up. She rubbed Rollie's back. "Nothing wrong with staying busy."

"All right, Ma, we—" Rollie said.

"The school need come up with some more programs like that. It's good to make y'all think about what you want do with your futures," she said, on a roll. "I'm glad TAG keeping him off the streets. It even got him out here auditioning for—"

Rollie cut her off. "All right, Ma, we gotta go." He pecked her on the cheek. "See you after practice."

He nudged Simp toward the door. Had that been G-ma, she would have laid him out for interrupting her. He thanked Him that it hadn't been. But he didn't want his mother talking about the Rowdy Boys band. It wasn't that he was keeping it from Simp. Not really. But the closer auditions came, the less he wanted to talk about it with him. He was nervous enough and couldn't take it if Simp teased him. Or worse, doubted him.

He'd told Mila. But that was different.

And, he'd almost told Chris. In the end, he knew there wouldn't have been any explaining that. So, he hadn't. He couldn't do Simp like that. And since *almost* didn't count, he was good.

Except, guilt nagged at him. He promised himself if Simp asked about it, right now, he'd fess up.

Only if he asked, though.

Their footsteps filled the silence until Simp blew his breath toward the sky. A puff of white drifted above their heads. "Mannn . . . we held it down at the J. Martins."

"No doubt," Rollie said. A warm trill ran down his back at the memory of Saturday's game.

Simp grinned at him. "Can't nobody stop us when we out there together. For real."

Rollie nodded, happy to let him go on.

"Ay, if I'm hard on you in practice or whatever, know I ain't tripping. All right?" He checked Rollie from the corner of his eye. "But you know Coach expect me handle mine. And that mean doing whatever to get us ready for the 'Peake. Know what I'm saying?"

"I ain't tripping off your little drills," Rollie said in mock irritation.

Simp burst out laughing. "Oh, you got jokes? Why my drills got be little?"

He stopped walking and they gripped. It felt like he held on a second longer than usual before he let go and busted back on Rollie.

"I bet your punk tail won't say that if I make you run grizzlies today."

Everybody hated grizzlies—six laps around the gym, three in a dead sprint and then three running backward. They were worse than sprint drills.

"Ohhh, that's just wrong," Rollie said.

The dissing went back and forth, growing louder as they neared the rec center.

Rollie couldn't remember the last time he'd felt this hopeful. Maybe if he just let it happen, everything would be all right.

SIMP

February wind wasn't no joke. It took his breath away as he stepped off the bus. The sixth and seventh graders beat feet around him, sprinting the one hundred yards to the nearest set of rows. He forced himself to slow down. It was cold, but he wasn't trying to look like some sucker running from the wind. Besides, he lived in fifth court. Nobody was running that much. He pulled the strings of his hood just as it was yanked off his head. Cappy rolled past him, laughing.

"You a punk, yo," Simp yelled after him.

"He really is," Tai said from beside him.

"He be acting like he in kindeegarden, sometimes,"

Simp muttered, tightening the hood to defeat the wind pushing at his back.

Tai laughed. "It's kin-der-gar-ten, Simp. Not kin-dee-gar-den."

He teased back. "When you get all proper? Bean giving you lessons or something?"

He waited for a typical Tai clap back—hands on hip, rolled eyes, sharp tongue. She surprised him by laughing. "I ain't hardly proper. But you sound crazy saying it wrong."

Simp slowed his pace, ignoring the cold stabbing at his face.

He wasn't sure what to say next without the squad around to fill the silence. Tai didn't have the same problem.

"You played real good at the J. Martins." She adjusted the muffs on her ears and picked up her pace. "I was hoping y'all would shut 'em down, too. Marcus big mouth wasn't running then."

The venom in her voice surprised him. She snorted at his side-eye. "I can't stand Marcus. He was out there saying some real foul mess about my father. And I don't need my name or my father's coming out his mouth."

Facts, Tai and her father didn't get along. Simp had

seen them get into it before. She hadn't looked one bit of afraid of him, either, going in on him like he was just some basic dude from off the streets and not her pops.

Another fact, Bryant, Tai's father, was a regular customer of Tez's crew. Simp had seen him drugged out plenty of times, walking the streets in his lazy swag like he hadn't slept for days. He guessed that's why Tai ain't have no love for him.

Either way, wasn't none of his business.

"Marcus always out there starting stuff," he said, plunging his hands into his pockets. He stayed talking like it was a warm June day as they arrived to Tai's front stoop. "You know he out there saying Rollie leaving the 'Rauders?"

Tai's mouth scrunched. "It figures. He gossip like a girl."

Simp laughed. "True shizz. True shizz."

Tai pushed him in the chest, gently. "Wait. I can say that 'cause I'm a girl. You can't."

He put his hands up in surrender. "Just agreeing with you."

"Rollie ain't going nowhere," she said, folding her arms. "We talk all the time and he ain't never say nothing about not balling no more."

She seemed so certain it made Simp jealous. He wished he could hit Tai up like that and talk about . . . whatever her and Rollie talked about so much. It also made him mad. Right after the J. Martins, Rollie was at every practice the next week. But now he was right back to rolling in late and had missed another Wednesday practice.

Simp had made him run extra sprint drills. If he hadn't, it would have looked like he was playing favorites.

How was Rollie too busy to make every practice but had time to hit Tai up?

Just then he remembered how Rollie's moms said something about him having auditions. How was he gonna be doing all that?

The answer was, he wasn't. He was slacking, and Simp was sick of it.

Tai was looking up at him, eyebrows knitted, head cocked. "You all right? Did you hear me?"

Simp looked away to give himself time to fix his face. "Naw. My bad. What you say?"

"I said he'd be crazy to quit the team right now. Y'all running things this year."

"No lies told," Simp said. "He brought that fire at

the J. Martins, for sure. But he gonna have to make up his mind sooner or later."

Tai wrapped her arms around herself against the cold. "About what?" She raised her eyebrow, a smile tugging at her mouth. "Y'all little side hustle?"

"Ain't nothing little 'bout our hustle," Simp said before he could stop himself. He took a step back. "Aight, look, I gotta dip."

Tai laughed. "Simp, it ain't like people don't know y'all work for Tez."

His face turned to stone. Simp was good at lying about the game: a) it wasn't nobody's business and b) first rule of the game is Don't talk about the game.

One time, when they first started working the front, Bean's father, Mr. Jamal, drove by. When his big black SUV slow rolled back, Simp knew he was in for a lecture or worse. He had been nervous. Mr. Jamal would call leecee on lookouts in a heartbeat.

By the time his window was down, Simp was ready for him.

"Ay, Mr. Jamal," he'd said, easy smile on his lips.

"What's up, Deontae? What you doing out here?" he'd asked, eyes scouting the area. But Simp was alone. Rollie had been at church that day—choir or something.

"Nothing. Just chilling," Simp had said. He forced himself to stay looking at Mr. Jamal. Everytime a car rode by, he'd pray it wasn't a customer and that he wasn't missing something. One, two, three cars rolled by as Mr. Jamal went on about how it looked bad when people just hung out near the neighborhood's entrance. If Simp didn't want people thinking he was doing wrong, then he should find something more "constructive" to do.

For real, if it had been anybody else, Simp would have mouthed off. But he was a little afraid of Mr. Jamal, and he also had mad respect for him. Mr. Jamal was always doing stuff to help people out. Every year he collected school supplies and made sure nobody was in school without notebooks and pencils. Simp and his brothers had needed some of the supplies once or twice till he started trapping. Now, he had them covered.

So, he couldn't be mad at Mr. Jamal. Everybody had their hustle. Mr. Jamal's was doing good. So, Simp had played along. Said he was waiting on his boys so they could walk up to the Wa. Mr. Jamal had squinted, like he was thinking whether to call Simp out for lying or naw. In the end, he had shaken his head side to side— like how people do when they know ain't no sense in going on—and told Simp to watch his self out there before driving off.

Simp had told Coach about the convo, and after that nobody was supposed to work alone anymore. A lot of times they'd all hang out at the fence together, whether it was their shift or not, just so it looked like they was just bulling and kicking it. Either all of 'em were dough boys or some were, but nobody really knew which ones. They was all each other's cover.

Tai was one of them people who was always trying to figure out who was down with the game. And Simp had a feeling she was probably cool with the hustle. The way her eyes lit with what else she wanted to say told him so. He still played it off. "You probably gon' go back and tell Rollie everything we said anyway, so go 'head and let him know he better stay on his grind before Cappy become the starter."

She rolled her eyes. "Cappy not as good as Rollie. And I'm not saying nothing. If you and Rollie beefing, y'all need work that out."

"Ain't nobody beefing," he said, uncertain.

Had she heard something?

"Then say what you just said to his face," Tai said, hands on her hips.

"I have," Simp said. Everything but that part about Cappy. But Tai didn't need to know that. "He know what's up if he keep missing practices."

"Um-hm, few seconds ago you wasn't talking about no basketball," Tai said with a snort.

"Bye, Metai," he said, walking off with her shouting at his back, "I know you ain't just full name me, Deontae."

He threw his hand up in a good-bye and picked up his pace. His legs were wobbly.

First rule of the game was Don't talk about the game. But, for a second, he had wanted to admit to Tai how deep in he was. He couldn't lie; part of it was to brag. Let her know about the money he had hidden. It wasn't the only thing, though. He wanted to feel like somebody was in it with him, knew his secret and was all right with it. 'Cause, for real, he didn't know if Rollie was still down. He kept saying he was but . . .

Simp shook off the doubt.

He needed to be around somebody who understood. He could have hit up anybody on the team, but as he walked to the row, he texted Rollie: *ay u should slide thru and let me beat up on you in Crown Battle.*

He stuffed the phone deep into his pocket, not

wanting to hold it in case Rollie didn't hit him back. Which would be messed up. But even more messed up if Rollie straight told him no.

Dom was watching some animal show on television. His eyes were glued to a big herd of elephants throwing dirt on their backs. Derek came racing downstairs making as much noise as the animals.

"My turn to pick something to watch," he yelled, standing dead in front of Dom. "You said I could pick once Simp got home."

Dom craned his neck around their younger brother and turned up the volume. Derek lunged at him to steal the remote.

Simp had his hoodie halfway off when the phone buzzed. He fought with the sweatshirt, his locs tangling in the fabric, anxious but scared to see the message.

Little Dee tackled his legs. He toppled back onto the sofa without crushing his baby brother as the hoodie finally let him loose.

"Let him watch something, Dom," Simp fussed.

"My show almost over," Dom said, never looking away from the TV.

"Where Dre?" Simp asked. He knew better than to

have Dee down here while Dom was zoning. Dee could have gotten into anything.

His brothers didn't answer.

"Thimp." Little Dee crawled into his lap and shoved a small car at him.

"What you want me do with this, man?" Simp asked, his voice gentle. He tucked Dee back on his lap in the crook of his arm as he dug out his phone. He ignored Derek's pleading that he make Dom give him the remote. Derek was a whiner, not a fighter, and Dom knew it. They could go on like that for as long as he let them.

Dee pushed the toy at Simp. "Car. Car." He rolled the car over Simp's leg and made car noises.

"Vrooom," Simp said absently as he finally looked down at Rollie's message: *Chris jus asked me come chill. Want roll?*

He couldn't think with Derek's whining. It was like a fire truck siren that wouldn't pass.

His voice rose. "Didn't I tell you give him the remote?"

His fist clenched, ready to punch Dom in the chest. Not enough to hurt him, just enough to remind him to do what he was told. But Dee wiggled in his arms and it made Simp look back down at the phone. A knot of black anger sat in his stomach. Rollie was going over Chris's to play video games, now?

The text had a grip on him.

He read it again and pulled the message apart like a doctor doing surgery.

Rollie had said Chris *just* invited him. So, they didn't have no set plans.

That made Simp feel better.

The other thing was, Rollie coulda lied and said he was busy or couldn't come out but he'd asked Simp to roll through.

Simp held on to that. He didn't really want kick it with Chris, but it was better than arguing with his brothers all day. Plus, the surprise on Chris's face when he busted in there with Rollie would make it worth it. Smug satisfaction melted the last of his anger.

Dee stood on Simp's lap and drove his car up the wall, his car noises a high-pitched babyfied hum.

"Dre, come here," Simp hollered. He texted around his baby brother: *yeah I slide thru.*

Dre took his time coming down the stairs. Of all their brothers, him and Dre were the only two that shared the small forehead, thanks to their deep hairline. But where

Simp's eyebrows were thick, Dre's were a tapered line. If Simp always looked confused, Dre's face had a constant look of expectation. He studied Simp, his face neutral, like he already knew what was coming.

"What?" he asked, leaning on the curve of the wall where the kitchen and living room separated.

Simp scowled. "What you mean, what?"

"You call me?" Dre said, with a little less bite.

Simp didn't mind the snap in Dre's voice. He'd taught him to stand up for himself and it was working. He plopped Dee beside Dom.

"I need run out." Simp automatically took a twenty-dollar bill out of his pocket and handed it to Dre. "Mommy be home soon."

Dre crushed the bill and stuck it in his pocket without looking at it.

"I'm sick of babysitting," he muttered under his breath.

"What you say?" Simp's eyebrow shot up. "If youn want it, give it back."

His hand was out but he wasn't expecting to have the crushed bill tossed back to him.

"Keep it then," Dre said. "I don't feel like dragging Dom to the Wa anyway."

At the mention of going outside, Dom frowned. "I don't feel like walking to the store. It's cold." He tossed the remote to Derek and grabbed a book sitting on the end table like it would anchor him in the house.

Simp's anger eased. Dre was salty because on top of not wanting to go outside, Dom hadn't felt like playing video games lately. And it was hard playing anything with Derek. He got mad too easily and threw tantrums.

It was like this 24-7. Everybody wanting to do what they wanted. Simp understood, but he wasn't about to let Dre get away with that much lip. He stared into Dre's eyes until his brother squirmed.

"I'mma crack your head next time you disrespect me," Simp said. He plucked the balled-up twenty-dollar bill, sending it flying into the kitchen. "Remember, Ioun gotta give you nothing. That bill still on the floor when I get back, you better be ready square up."

Dre's chin quivered as he talked. "Why I gotta always stay here? Dom can watch Derek and Dee sometimes. He old enough." He swiped angrily at the tears rolling down his face. "How come I can't never go with you?"

"I be taking care of business," Simp said, feeling bad for the lie.

"I could still go with you. I wouldn't get in the way or nothing," Dre said.

The hope in his voice tore Simp up. He could have easily hit Rollie up and told him he'd kick it another time. Rollie probably wouldn't care either way, and that's what spurred him on.

Dre would be fine. Everybody getting their way wasn't how it was.

"Man, look, you can't come with me. All right?" Simp said. "You next up. That's just how it is. Moms be—"

Dre's arms folded as he went into a full pout. "Mommy ain't even here half the time. You be leaving and saying she be home soon, but she never is."

At that, Derek panicked. "Who gonna cook us something to eat?"

His big brown eyes searched his brothers for answers.

It was too much for Simp. All he wanted to do was get out and kick it with Rollie for a little bit. Kick it like they used to before TAG and Chris.

He felt like wild'n out on his brothers, remind them that none of this was his fault. He was doing the best he could.

Dre's voice shook with emotion. "I look like a lame always locked up in the house. Then Mommy don't even let me have company over talking 'bout she don't need people messing up the house."

It broke Simp. He couldn't blow up on his little man. He knew how Dre felt. It wasn't their fault that they had to stay cooped up in the house all the time. Derek got into too much when he was outside. Dee was too young to be outside, and Dom didn't like going outside anymore. They didn't have no choice but to drive each other nuts in the house waiting on their mother to deliver on her fake promises of going this place or that once she got home.

The whole thing ran Simp hot at their mother. She acted like just because she went to work every day to pay rent and buy groceries, that her job was done. Like he wasn't out there making scrilla and bringing it home, too. But he ain't never get to escape. Why should she?

He couldn't say all that, though. Dre was upset, but he was also a momma's boy. Their mother could find out any and everything they'd all said while she was gone by sweet-talking him.

"You know how moms is," was all Simp would say.

It wasn't a defense. It wasn't even no excuse. It was

just the truth. He didn't have no promises to make to Dre. Except . . .

"Look, you keeping your grades up right?" he asked.

Dre's mouth pooched like he had no idea what that had to do with anything, but he answered, "Yeah."

"All right, that mean you can try out for 'Rauders in the spring. Coach said I can bring you to a practice. Let you work out with the team. All right?"

Later, all Simp could think about was how Dre's eyes had lit up. He hadn't thanked Simp or even responded to him. But he'd gotten up, grabbed a game controller, and invited Derek to play *Crown Battle*. A fighting game their mother hated. She said it was too violent. But she wasn't there, was she?

That's what it was.

They was all just trying to get by.

ROLLIE

The hits kept coming.

A kick. A punch.

Rollie weaved as flames flew over his head. He charged and stunned his opponent with a blue streak of power. With a few seconds to spare, he reached in for the kill. His impossibly huge muscles rippled with the effort.

He kept up the pressure—kick, kick, jab.

"Son, you got him. You got him," Simp said. He paced beside the couch. "Finish him."

Rollie blocked out the sounds of real life and became the hulking character on the screen. He slid across the arena, fury in his eyes and his limbs, pummeling his opponent until two huge letters floated on the screen: KO.

"Ahhhh man," Chris yelled. His character, a burly green-faced giant with a lion's mane, fell to the ground defeated.

"Yessssss," Simp howled. "You merked him." He dapped Rollie up. "Get those weak moves outta here, yo. Rollie whipped that ass."

Rollie and Chris slid their hands and gripped at the end. "Good game. You almost had me, though," Rollie said. He brought his voice down, trying to signal to Simp to chill. Chris's mom wasn't home but Chrissy was. She probably thought they were down here fighting for real the way Simp was going off.

Simp stabbed at the television, voice still bassing. "He ain't almost have nothing. You owned him."

The game controller hung lazily in Chris's hand as he dangled it in Simp's general direction. "Show and prove, then."

Simp snatched it and kept jawing. "You ain't said nothing, partner."

Rollie stood up and stretched. "I need a break. Here." He handed his controller to Chris. "Y'all two get at it."

He met Simp's confused gaze with a shrug as he took a seat off to the side of the sofa. He knew Simp probably didn't want to play Chris again. They'd been having a good time, chilling and playing the game, until Chris had beat Simp. Ever since, Simp had poured all his energy into being Rollie's personal cheerleader. Rollie had only beaten Chris by concentrating like his life depended on winning. The whole thing gave him a headache. Now he regretted not asking Simp why he had wanted to come along.

Chris was cool peoples. Simp's determination not to get along with him made Rollie feel like a referee. It was played out. He was glad when Chrissy came down the stairs. She was tall and thin and kept her hair in a fat, high bun that made her look taller. She was the total opposite of her brother, who was built thick like he had recently lost weight and was about Rollie's height. For being twins they barely looked alike except their almond brown skin and large, round brown eyes.

He liked Chrissy. She wasn't loud like Metai or ready for every fight like Mo, but he'd seen her carry Tai with a simple comeback without ever raising her voice. That was another way her and her twin were alike. But if Rollie was honest, he liked her because

Mila liked her. And he trusted Mila. Plain and simple.

In the Cove trust was everything.

"What's up, Christol," he said, happy for the distraction.

"Hey," she said, with a polite smile that brightened when she looked at Simp. "Hey, Deontae. You know you owe me one more Pong lesson, right?"

"We need hurry up and get this stupid bet over with," Simp said, practically growling. He gave Rollie an exasperated look. "We gonna be having practice every day till the 'Peake. It's gonna be hard for me keep doing this."

"So, you talking to me or Chrissy?" Rollie asked, annoyed.

"Just saying," Simp said.

"Dang, you called the bet stupid," Chrissy said, hands on her hips. "Boy, this for bragging rights up in here. This bet is for real, for real."

Rollie was glad Simp had the good sense to look embarrassed. His respect for Chrissy went up another notch.

"The bet *is* stupid," Chris said with an eye roll. "But I'm just waiting on y'all. We can do it whenever."

Simp stood up and dropped the controller on the

couch. Rollie reluctantly readied himself to roll out with him.

"Ay, Chrissy, let's head to the rec to practice then," Simp said. "Ain't no difference in me whipping up on him on this game or teaching you to do it in Ping-Pong."

"Now?" Chrissy asked. A tiny smile dimpled her cheeks.

Simp nodded. "Might as well."

"Let me get my shoes on," Chrissy said.

Simp walked over and knocked fists lightly with Rollie. "All right. I holler later." He camped out by the door. His head was too deep in his hoodie for Rollie to see his face, but he knew Simp was mad. Lately, he always was.

For the last week, Rollie had worked harder to make practices. On time. On top of that, he had even stayed thirty minutes longer last time they worked the front. It had made him late for choir rehearsal and he'd heard it from his grandmother that whole night. All so Simp could stop checking on him and his "loyalty." And none of it mattered.

If anything, Simp had been even more intense at practice, calling extra drills and correcting people's form like he was the coach. Dude was turning into Tiny

Tez. It took everything for Rollie not to call him out. But once practice was over he'd go home, pull up a clip of his audition piece, and air drum until his limbs ached from the effort. Basketball was basketball. Music was music. He wasn't letting one interfere with the other anymore. Keeping them apart was his new hustle.

His jaw gripped as Chris kept things going.

"Don't forget this y'all last practice," he said.

"Man, I know," Simp said, yelling.

At some point, Rollie would have to jump in to chill it out even though this wasn't his fight. And jumping in would only start a new beef or worse.

Simp had a good three or four inches on Chris. But Chris had at least twenty pounds on Simp. Simp could throw hands, for sure. But, Rollie had a feeling if it got physical, it would be a draw. He wished Chrissy would hurry up. He pretended to be checking messages on his phone as Chris baited Simp.

"Just making sure you know." Chris smirked. "I mean, I'm up for it if you want us just get the game over with now. But if you think one more practice gonna do something—"

"Son, you not that good. Trust, I got this. She gonna beat you," Simp said. His hands were sunk so deep in his hoodie pocket that Rollie could see the imprint of his fists.

Thankfully, Chrissy came stomping down the stairs. She joined the conversation like it had hung in the air paused. "And for your information, Chris, I am getting better." She looked at Simp for confirmation.

"I already told him you got this," Simp said.

"Then what you need one more practice for?" Chris asked. He turned his face back to the TV and scrolled through the characters.

"'Cause you gave us three pun . . . " For a beat Simp was silent. When he started talking again, his body was more relaxed like he'd clicked some button. "The bet was I could get her to beat you with only three practices. So, what? You want change the rules or back out now?"

Chris laughed. "It ain't even that serious. Be home before Momma, Chrissy."

She waved, unfazed, and grabbed Simp by the wrist. A cold draft rushed in as they opened the door on the darkening day. It lingered around Rollie's feet long after the door was shut.

"Man, your boy gots no chill," Chris said. He nodded to the controller Simp had left. "We still playing?"

Rollie eased over to the sofa and picked up the chunk of plastic. It was warm in his hands. His fingers rolled over the raised buttons. Chris hadn't asked him a question, but he had just dissed Simp. It felt wrong leaving it out there.

"Nah, he got chill. He just don't like you, son," he said.

Chris's loud laughter infected him. They scrolled through the screen, setting up the next game, their laughter melting away the weight that had pushed Rollie into the floor.

"I ain't even tripping over it," Chris said. "But since we talking real, I need ask you something." He locked eyes with Rollie. "Is your boy in the dope game?"

Rollie's face went hot. He cupped at his chin like he was pulling at a thatch of hair and forced himself to frown. "Why you asking?"

Chris held his gaze one more second then talked at the television. "'Cause I ain't stupid and it seem like my sister like that knucklehead." He shook his head. "I don't know why, but she do. She always saying how nice he is and how he funny."

Rollie happily let Chris talk on until his words could catch up with his thoughts.

"I ain't trying have my sister caught up with no dude who trappin'." Chris sighed. "Look, yo, I ain't trying preach on you or whatever. He your buddy and what he do—that's his business. But once this bet over, my sister don't need be spending time with him. I don't want nothing pop off and she caught in the middle."

"I know you and him don't get along, but for real, Simp the most loyal dude I know," Rollie said. The truth in that made him feel bad for how desperately he'd wanted to shove Simp out the door to prevent him and Chris from getting into it. Because he knew that if he had to choose, right then and there, he would have been on Chris's side. He would have sided against his best friend.

The thought made him sick.

He sat up until he was on the edge of the couch. He couldn't make Chris like Simp. He didn't even care about that anymore. But he couldn't let Chris think Simp was dangerous. "Keeping it one hundred, I think he don't like you 'cause he not sure he can trust you, yet. It's just how he is."

Rollie saw Chris thinking it over. "When he gets to know you, he has your back. Chrissy be all right with him."

"Cool. But you still ain't say if he trappin or not." When Rollie went silent, Chris let him off the hook a little. "We only known each other a minute and Simp *been* your boy. So, I'm probably out of pocket. But that's my sister. Know what I'm saying?"

Once again, his wide brown eyes fixed on Rollie, waiting for an answer. An answer Rollie couldn't give him. He had never admitted to anybody that he was one of Tez's dough boys. Never. He'd come close with Tai once, only because she brought it up every other conversation. She was fascinated with it and made it clear it was cool with her if he was. But Tez had been a good teacher. He didn't talk about the hustle with anybody not in the game.

It wasn't that people didn't suspect. But suspicions were like opinions; everybody had one. It definitely wasn't something you just asked somebody. Not even about somebody else.

"I hear you. But if you want know something about Simp, you need ask him," Rollie said, forcing the words out over his drying mouth. He gathered the last ounce of courage he had to meet Chris's intense gaze. "Know what I'm saying?"

A hardness came over Chris's face that Rollie had

never seen before. He wanted to take his words back. Wanted to go back to the first time they'd met and realized they had music in common. He was lying to Chris, and somehow Chris knew it.

In the next instant, Chris's face was blank. "You right. That's on me."

He looked straight ahead at the screen. His fingers clicked a button on the controller and the television growled, "Fight."

Rollie woodenly obeyed.

SIMP

Chrissy was pushing up against him.

Simp pressed in, wanting to explore. She raised her arm to serve the ball and the roundness of her butt pulled away, just enough to make Simp want to jerk forward and close the gap. Then just as quickly, she hit the ball and was back on him pressing gently but enough to—

His mother's voice yanked him out of the dream.

"Deontae. Deontae, get up."

He sat up, half his mind still in the dream, and slammed his back against the headboard to jolt himself into the present. The tension in his groin was so tight no way his mother didn't see the tent in his sheet. How long had she been standing there? Had he been moaning? A mixture of anger and guilt gave him the courage to yell back, "I'm up, Ma. Dang."

He just wanted her yapping to stop. Calling his name like it was going out of style or something.

"Don't you cuss at me, boy," she said, determined to get the upper hand in an argument he didn't feel like having. He didn't hear anger in her voice. He took his chances and lipped back.

"'Dang' ain't cussing. Did you wake me up just to fight with me?"

"No. I need talk to you," she said.

Simp picked up his phone, staring at the time. "It's only eight o'clock, Ma. Dang."

She pursed her lips. "I know that. It's important, Deontae. Meet me downstairs." She took a step then paused, eyes narrowed. "You can go back to your little nasty dream later."

Her laughter rang in the narrow hallway.

Simp threw the sheets off. His mother was wild. He wouldn't have been able to go back to the dream if he wanted to now. He pulled on a T-shirt and quietly made his way down the stairs.

The smell of bacon pulled him the rest of the way. Every seat at the rickety fake wood table was open, but he sat in his seat—the only chair with its back to the kitchen wall. From there he could see if anyone came through the kitchen's back door or the living room's front door. Only suckers sat with their backs to a door.

His mother was at the stove, nudging at the bacon in the frying pan.

"What's up, Ma?" He fought a yawn and swiped at random locs spilling into his face. Getting him up early was one thing, but his mother was cooking. He wondered how much she wanted this time.

Sure enough, she turned on the sugar and her voice lost its usual sharp edge.

"It's about your brothers."

What was he ready to be blamed for now? A bad grade? Did somebody get into a fight at school? He clamped his mouth shut. If he was gonna get blamed for something, she was just gonna have to lay it out.

His mother's smile became a dissatisfied tight line. She gave him another second but Simp remained quiet. She rolled her eyes, snatching a piece of bacon out of the pan and slapping it onto a paper towel. "Look,

Deontae, Dre old enough to start playing for Tez. And Dom is close."

Again, she stopped, as if waiting on him to magically fill in the blanks. All Simp would offer was, "Yeah."

"Yeah," she spit back. "So, you're the captain this year. The captain holds weight on who might be on the come up." Her free hand clamped down on her hip. "Are you going to put your little brothers on?"

It smacked him in the face to hear her use the words "put on." If all she wanted Dre to do was get out the house, he could have been playing for the Cougars years ago. He didn't need to be "put on" to nothing just to play ball.

This wasn't about no basketball.

A few seconds before, the greasy smell of bacon had him thinking of slapping it between two slices of toast. Now it made him want to open a door and let in some air.

"Dom too young. He only nine. Plus, you gotta be in sixth grade," he said, unable to look at her.

She waved the fork, like a wand. "But Dre not. If his stupid ass get it together, he'll be in sixth grade next year."

Simp's jaw clenched. "Don't call him stupid, Ma."

"Boy, that child came out of me. I call him what I want." She eased the rest of the bacon onto the paper towel, dabbing at them more gently than she ever did anything else. She clicked the stove off, brought the plate of bacon over like it was an offering. "Here. I made you breakfast."

Simp started to say bacon wasn't much of a breakfast. But for his mother, it was more than she usually did on a Saturday morning. He muttered, "Thanks," but couldn't bring himself to touch it.

She sipped coffee from a black mug with "Number One Mom" in big white letters on it. Derek had bought it from the dollar store last Mother's Day. The words made Simp's head hurt. At least Derek was only seven. He had a minute before he had to worry about this.

He talked toward the crispy strips of pork. "What you want me do, Ma?"

The sugar was back.

"Tez obviously like you. I'm just saying put in a good word for your brothers. They can't sit around the house playing video games forever." She crossed her arms. "You not gonna eat after I cooked for you?"

"I'm still trying get up, for real," he said, forcing his eyes upward.

For the longest, he had done what he could to keep his brothers from getting in trouble. But school, basketball, and hustling meant he wasn't home as much. Getting Dre and Dom onto the Marauders would mean giving them a break from their mother. And it meant making cash. That's what his mother cared about.

He pushed himself away from the table and busied himself making toast. Anything so he wouldn't have to look at her.

"Ioun even think Dom like basketball, for real. He a nerd," he said, putting respect on the word. Dom was smart. Real smart.

He heard the frown in her voice. "Then he can be the water boy, Deontae. I don't care." The softness edged in and out. "Dre is good, though. The only reason he not on the team this year is because he failed fifth grade. When he get in middle school, I know Tez won't sleep on his skills."

Simp hated that his mother knew all that. How long had she been thinking about this?

His brain slow rolled over it all. He couldn't take the facts apart and put them back together fast enough to respond the way he wanted to. Instead, he stared down into the toaster. The coils burned orange, mesmerizing him.

He knew his mother's eyes were on him and he'd have to say something or do something. He was the man of the house.

I could say no, he thought.

Everybody wasn't cut out to hustle. Dom wasn't. But Dre . . . even Coach Tez thought he was ready. Maybe it was time. The reality of it cut into him.

"Deontae."

His mother's voice raked over his nerves, but snapped him out of what he'd been thinking.

Dre wasn't ready. That's what it was.

He flipped the toaster's handle, forcing the toast up, snatched the bread, and joined her at the table. Her lips were pursed, ready to argue. He wanted to ask her why she was doing this. Wasn't one of them in the game enough?

His jaw clenched so hard it hurt. He grit his teeth against the anger tearing at his throat. There was shouting in his head, things he wanted to say to his mother. Instead, he slipped one piece of bacon off the plate. Broke it in half and laid it across the bread.

He waited for her to say something, but she played his game and stayed quiet.

He slipped another piece of bacon off the plate

and placed it down. The bacon looked like soldiers, shoulder-to-shoulder. He put the other piece of bread on top. Sometimes he said grace before he ate. Sometimes he didn't. He only knew one anyway— "God is great, God is good and we thank him for this food. Amen."

He closed his eyes against his mother's unblinking gaze. In another second she was going to blow. He felt it. Saw that her mouth was back to the tight line. He breathed slowly through his nose, letting it settle his heart. "Forgive me," he whispered before saying the grace he'd learned at some vacation bible school a million years ago.

When he looked up, his mother's face was tight but expectant. Then it was like she saw inside him, past his worries. She broke into a smile, gushing, "You a good boy. I know you gonna watch out for your brothers."

He put the sandwich up to his mouth, put it back down. "I'm only gon' get Dre on the team. Nobody got time to be watching over Dom." He cleared his throat over the lump. "Somebody got watch Dee anyway while we at practice and shi . . . stuff."

He doubted it would have mattered if he'd cussed. His mother had gotten what she wanted. She was on to the next, up and dumping the bacon grease into an empty can. "We worry about Dom later. We got time," she said.

"We."

Simp chewed slowly, trying his best to get the bacon down his gullet. It was like chewing on a shoe.

"We" was still on his mind as he got dressed later for his shift. He talked himself through all of the details.

Tryouts were in April. If Dom passed fifth grade, he'd make the team, period, 'cause he knew how to handle the rock. And whether Simp liked it or not, he couldn't control how Tez used him off the court. All he could do was get Dre ready.

He burped up bacon as his stomach churned at the thought: He was really gonna put his little brother on.

He closed his eyes until the throbbing in his head dulled.

He had to do what he had to do. If anybody was going to hip his brother to the game, it had to be him. That's what it was.

He was pulling his kicks on when his phone buzzed. He ignored it, figuring it was Rollie wondering where he was.

A black mark had the nerve to be on his clean white

shoes. Time to give these to Dre, he thought, kicking the shoe off. He finally picked up the phone and grinned at the text from Chrissy.

Chriss-E: *Hey. You up?* ●●

He answered—*Yup*—then went into his closet and grabbed a newish pair of kicks from one of the fifty boxes he had in order by style and color. Always J's. Most of 'em basketball shoes from Tez, but he'd treated himself to a few dozen. Some hadn't been worn yet.

He glanced down at the phone and his smile died.

Chriss-E: *Is it true that you deal drugs?*

Simp's head reared back. Was shorty for real?

He took his time getting his shoes on as he fought the tight annoyance in his chest. He wrote a note on the box with the scuffed pair inside—*Dre, don't ever say I ain't give u nothin*—then dropped it inside the room his younger brothers shared.

He threw a woolie on his head and pulled it down to his ears as best as he could over his thick locs. His phone buzzed, a fury of back-to-back messages.

"I be back later," he yelled to anyone who cared.

He took a few steps before stopping to check the messages.

Chriss-E: *Hello?*

Chriss-E: *Not trying be in ur business. But . . . can u be real w/me?*

Chriss-E: *Can u call me at least? Chris kind of buggin'* 😫

Seeing Chris's name got his fingers sliding across the phone, dialing her number. He met her breathless "Hello" with silence. "Hello," she said again, sounding confused.

Simp couldn't believe he was calling her about this. He looked up the street toward the rec center, half expecting Coach Tez to be standing watch over him. But the community was still quiet. Only a few people were out scurrying to their cars out of the cold. He forced his voice to sound unconcerned. "Yeah. What's up?"

"You know what's up," she said, whispering.

"For real, I don't though," he said. He started a slow walk toward the mouth of the hood. It wasn't as cold as it had been the week before, but he punched his free hand into his hoodie pocket, needing to do something with himself to stay under control. He opened and flexed his fist as she talked.

"I mean, can you answer my question," she said.

"Ay, look, Iouno how they get down where y'all from, but you lunchin' a lil' bit," Simp said, with as much patience as he could. His jaw shivered from holding it so tight. Coach Tez would flip if he knew he was talking about this and to some random shorty at that. He took the phone off his ear and deleted Chrissy's text messages as her voice questioned him. Without even knowing what she'd said, he jumped back on, talking over her. "We cool, but you don't know me like that."

"I mean, but you not denying it, either," she said.

He stamped out the guilt creeping up on him with advice from Coach Tez—*Ain't nothing bigger than the game. But people gon' try convince you otherwise.*

His grind wasn't none of Chrissy's business. The cold whipped at his face as he picked up speed. "First off, I ain't saying nothing either way. All I'm saying is you don't know me like that. You can't just be asking people stuff like that."

He could hear somebody in the background muffled like she had the phone far away from the sound. She spoke to the person then came back firm, like either she'd shut her door or was sure whoever had been there was gone.

"I wasn't trying to make you mad. And I guess I probably shouldn't have came at you like that," she said.

He couldn't help smiling, especially when she

continued, "I can't get an apology accepted?"

"I ain't never hear I'm sorry," he said, chuckling.

He looked around the quiet neighborhood, glad nobody was watching him be a straight sucker on the phone. Tez was always warning them against falling for the boo trap and letting a girl take them off their hustle. He'd never had that problem before and wasn't trying get caught up over no shorty, but—her laugh in his ear felt good.

"I'm sorry I came off wrong," Chrissy said.

The rickety wooden fence came into view. Rollie was already there, perched, his head down, looking at his phone. Simp stopped and pushed the conversation along. "It's all right. I mean . . . it's not. But we good."

"Okay good. But look—Chris . . ." There was a loud breath on her end. "For some reason, Chris think you doing something, and he said now that you finished coaching me in Ping-Pong he don't want me hang with you by myself anymore."

Simp snorted. "What, he your father or something?"

"Sometimes he think so," she said.

"Ay, I ain't trying cause no sibling rivalry or whatever," Simp said, laughing at his own dumb joke. "Just saying, what you want me do? If you want chill with me, then we can chill. But if your brother ain't down with it and you rock wit' it, then I rock wit it, too."

Her answer was rushed and back to a whisper. "I don't want to rock with it, though. Still, if you . . . you know—doing anything—then he said that's just trouble."

Simp was close to telling her how he felt about her brother, but that was between him and Chris. "All right, well, I gotta dip," he said.

"Is that it?" she asked.

"For real, what you want me do?" he asked.

"Nothing, Deontae," she said, finally. "Talk to you later."

He said "all right" but she was already gone.

He jammed the phone into his hoodie pocket, gripping it hard enough to bite into his flesh. His stomach felt like it was full of hot nickels. He hawked and spit off to the side as he walked up to the fence.

Rollie put his hand out for dap.

Simp absently slapped his hand against Rollie's twice and they gripped at the fingers. He climbed onto the fence next to him and let one, two, then three cars roll by before he turned to Rollie and said, "What you and Chris talk about after me and Chrissy left the other day?"

He stared into Rollie's face, looking for a squint or frown. Rollie's head ticked side to side. "We ain't talk about nothing, really. He was too busy whipping up on me in *Crown Battle*."

Simp worked hard to stop his whole body from clenching like a fist.

"Y'all ain't talk at all?" he asked, looking out at the road. He listened for the lie.

"I ain't saying we didn't talk. Just saying we ain't talk about nothing I remember," Rollie said.

"So, you ain't tell him me and you was in the game?" Simp asked. He popped off the fence and paced.

"There you go," Rollie said, eyes rolling.

"There I go, what? You musta said something, son," Simp said.

Rollie's cheeks sucked in, out, then back in until he had fish lips. He gazed down the street, all the time shaking his head denying. He stepped down from the fence and stood face-to-face with Simp.

"That's messed up, son," he said.

"I'm saying . . . you musta said something," Simp said, less convinced.

"Why?" Rollie asked. He looked to the left for a few seconds then his right, keeping watch as they spoke.

"'Cause Chrissy just called and asked me did I deal drugs," Simp said.

"So that means I said something to Chris?" Rollie asked. He put his hands up in question. "For real, yo?"

"I ain't stupid, Rollie. You musta said something," Simp said. But he didn't know anymore. Just like this morning, the conversation was moving too fast.

Simp wanted to apologize. Take it all back. He just wished he could be sure. He tried again.

"I'm saying, maybe you said something and Chris took it the wrong way," Simp said.

Rollie climbed back onto the fence. He pulled his cap down until it covered his eyebrows. His head moved back and forth so slow Simp wondered if he was zoning to a beat.

"Look—" Simp started.

Rollie put his hand up. "Naw, it's good. You said what you meant. I'm a rat."

Simp joined him on the fence, desperate to take it all back. "Man, I ain't say all that. If it's a coincidence, my bad. But, son, she texted me that mess. It got me twisted. I just—"

"I said it's good, son. Let it rock," Rollie said.

Simp tried to make the vibe between them right.

"How you just gonna text somebody something like that? I told her that's not how we do over here." He saw the slow nod of Rollie's head from the side of his eye. "If Chris want know so bad, why he ain't step to me?" His hollow chuckle was mean. "But he got good sense. Know what I'm saying?"

Rollie's simple nod dried up the words wanting to stream out of Simp's mouth.

They sat in the cold silence until Rollie stepped down.

"Look, I got do something for my grandmother. You good to finish without me?"

Already facing the direction that would take him home, he wasn't asking for permission. Simp expected him to walk off with or without an answer. But Rollie stood there, looking off into the distance, waiting on Simp's eventual nod. With a barely audible "cool," he left Simp staring at his back.

ROLLIE

"So, what happened with you and Simp?"

Tai's tinny voice nagged from the laptop speaker. She gazed straight into the cam, expecting an answer. He didn't know the answer to give. Nothing "happened" between him and Simp. Nothing that he was going to tell her about anyway.

He hated that she acted like she was somebody's mother, sometimes. He cast his eyes downward as his phone lit up with a message from Mila.

JahMeeLah: *even if u leave the Cove it never lets u go. learned that the hard way last summer* 😞

Rollie couldn't argue. He played drums at church

and that hadn't changed anything. He'd gotten into TAG and it hadn't mattered. Even if he made it into the Rowdy Boys, it probably still wouldn't make a difference. Because nothing ever did.

No matter what he did, he still had to have Simp's back. Tez's back. The hood's back.

"Hello? You still there?" Tai asked.

He tapped off a message to Mila—*that's real messed up*—then put his face back into view of his cam.

"What do you keep doing? Your head disappearing in and out making me seasick," Tai said. She peered at the screen, trying to see past the tiny bubble of the camera lens.

"My bad. I'm trying do homework," he said.

"Oh. Why you talking to me then?" she asked, with a big grin.

"You hit me up," he reminded her, with an eyebrow flick. She loved being the center of attention anytime they talked. He couldn't lie—he was all right with it, sometimes. He was definitely all right with how she'd be all up on him, standing close enough so her butt was touching his hip or leg—yeah, he liked that. But he wasn't looking for no girlfriend. He hated when she acted like she owned him, side-eyeing anytime he had words for another girl.

He glanced as his phone's backlight beckoned him again.

JahMeeLah: *it is but it doesn't mean u can't keep trying to get out. u know? U still got ur audition.* ☺ On cue, Tai's voice demanded his attention. "For real, if you got homework to do I'mma let you go, 'cause you not even talking."

He started to say "all right then" and let her go so he could focus on texting Mila, but he hadn't answered Tai's original question and he needed to squash mess before it got too deep in the rumors.

"Nah, I'm good. Go 'head," he said, inviting her to go back to what she really wanted to talk about in the first place.

Her eyebrows furrowed. "You and Simp beefing or something? Y'all wasn't talking at the bus stop, and on the way home he said something about Chris starting stuff."

Rollie's lip twitched as he stopped himself from reacting. He wiped at his mouth to get his face in order. "Naw, we not beefing. He don't like Chris." He shrugged. "And Chris don't like him. I'm caught in the middle and it's played out. That's all and that's it."

He tapped out a message to Mila as Tai talked: *I am*

focused on it but for real everybody trying be up in what I should do and how I should do it. Like be off me 😠

"Not trying take sides but you did kind of drop Simp once Chris moved here," Tai said.

Rollie frowned at her face in the small square box on his screen. "I dropped him? You act like he was my girlfriend or something."

"I hope the girlfriend position already filled." She laughed. "But for real, you do hang out with Chris a lot now. You know you was Simp's ace." She pinched her fingers close together. "He just a lil' salty."

Rollie palmed his phone off to the side of the screen to read Mila's message: *fr fr I'm not saying its easy. When I'm in dance that's all I'm thinking about tho. I think I might get a solo for the spring showcase* 🤞

"Hold up," Rollie said to Tai. He typed in full view of the cam: *Ay shout out to that!* 🐦 🎉 *u killing it*

"I know you not texting some other chick while I'm right here," Tai said, arms crossed.

It was so crazy that she jumped right to that. Crazier that she was right. He played it off smooth. "Nah. But look, me and Simp be all right. I gotta handle mines right now, though."

Her face took over the camera. "Meaning?"

He leaned back, raising the front of his chair off the floor. It made it easier to keep his face forward but glance over in case his phone flashed.

"Meaning, I got some business to take care of first. Then it's whatever whatever with Simp. Like I said, we fine," he said.

"Rollie, don't mess around and get cut from the team. It's bad enough you not co-captain," Tai said, doing her pouty thing.

"I got this," he said, practically growling.

She rolled her eyes. "Look, I was just trying help y'all out. When me and Bean—" She sucked her teeth. "When me and Mila wasn't talking over the summer, it sucked. Chris is cool. But you and Simp been friends too long to be tripping."

"You done, Dr. Tai?" Rollie asked, eyebrows raised.

"Yeah. But I'm serious. Do whatever dudes do to squash a beef. I mean, if I can be cool with Chrissy—" Her shoulder popped in a shrug. "Anything possible, these days."

"You got it," he said. "I need go, all right?"

Instead of saying bye, Tai struck a kissy face pose. She always wanted the camera to catch her looking fly. Rollie hung up, laughing.

He wasn't mad at Tai for playing peacemaker. He liked how close the squad had gotten since summer, too. Once the audition was over, he would have more time to think about getting Simp and Chris to chill out their differences. For now, he slid buds in his ear, laid back on the bed, and air drummed to the music.

Too bad that wasn't enough.

Weeks of practice. Sore arms from beating both imaginary and real drums and he wasn't ready. Not even a little bit. Why did he think he could do this?

Rollie's heart thumped in his ears, making it hard to understand what Mr. B was saying. He nodded along until he realized the sounds coming from his teacher's mouth had stopped. Mr. B was squinting at him, saying something. Rollie widened his eyes and thankfully his ears popped.

He caught the tail end of Mr. B's question: "All right?" He was ready to lie but couldn't even do that. He'd lost every ounce of chill he ever had.

"I'm scared," Rollie said, his legs melting under him.

"I'd be worried if you weren't," Mr. B said. His hand

clamped gently onto Rollie's shoulder, steadying him. "Listen to me for a second. There's nothing wrong with being scared of the unknown. You hear me?"

Mr. B's hand gripped just a little tighter. "Fear can be good." He smiled at Rollie's confused frown. "I'm serious. Fear is an instinct. It can keep you alive, make you run from that strange sound or that person who doesn't seem quite right coming toward you. It's a feeling coursing through your body telling you to pay attention—do something." He patted Rollie's shoulder. "Since you're not in danger, use your fear to pound that beat out with as much energy as you can. Use it, Roland."

Rollie's breath eased. He rested on the wall and used it to stand up straighter.

The door across from them opened. The dude that came out was short and round, like he enjoyed a good meal three times a day, maybe four. He rocked an all-brown velvet tracksuit and a pair of all white J's. It made him look like a walking teddy bear. Even more when his face lit into a smile.

His hand was already out as soon as he saw Mr. B.

"What's up, Pee Wee?" Mr. B said, going in for a pound and hug.

They thumped each other's back for a good minute before Pee Wee let go.

"Man, you looking good," he said to Mr. B. He patted at his own velvety soft mid-section. "Look at you still at your playing weight."

They laughed. "I never could gain weight. That's why I went into music. Y'all was starting to bust me up on the court throwing bows and what not," Mr. B said. He interrupted their trip down memory lane. "This is Roland Matthews. I told you, he's one of my star students in the county's new talented and gifted program."

Rollie shook Pee Wee's outstretched hand. His tongue was still mute.

"I still can't believe you a teacher," Pee Wee said. He smiled over at Rollie. "Man, this cat used to prank teachers all the time. He better hope ain't no get back waiting for him."

Mr. B's laugh was a deeper baritone than usual. "Man, don't wish that on me. My students are good kids. I don't need them knowing about my past." He pushed Rollie forward a bit. "I appreciate you giving Roland a tryout. He straight raw talent. Could be a good fit."

The words slammed into Rollie's ears and wrapped around his chest. He wanted to hug Mr. B and hold on for a minute until the tingling nerves left his arms and legs.

Pee Wee moved him along. "I trust your ear, Bones."

At that Rollie laughed, jangling free from the nerves. The nickname was perfect. Rollie didn't have a hood nickname. And he wasn't mad. It could be real messed up to end up with a name like Lockjaw or Pork Chop. But watching Pee Wee (who had been small at some point, maybe?) and Bones kicking it like they were still back in the day calmed him.

"Friends always tell your business," Mr. B said with a sad shake of his head. "Go on and show 'em what you got, Roland."

With Pee Wee's hand on his back, Rollie was gently nudged toward the darkened studio. He didn't know if the whole Rowdy Boys band was inside waiting or what. Strains of the song he'd been living and breathing played, pulling him its way.

He took a breath and walked inside.

The studios at school were that in name only. They were classrooms without desks. Chairs were usually scattered around the room and there was space, with a platform, for a small group of students playing instruments. This was a real studio. Inside the control room was a huge soundboard in front of a glass facing several mic stands and a drum set in the room across from it.

Rollie's stomach shriveled. He followed Pee Wee into the empty room.

"Go ahead and warm up, while I check the levels," Pee Wee said, not bothering to wait for an answer.

Rollie sat down behind the drums. They were nicer than the school's set. Nicer than the church's. The silver rimming each drum glistened against the set's deep burgundy color. He stroked the top of them, letting the coolness calm his shaking hands. For a second he forgot he was in an audition. He was excited to see what these drums felt like.

He pulled drum sticks out of his bag before sliding it into a corner.

He jumped at Pee Wee's voice coming through the PA overhead. "Throw your hand up when you ready."

Rollie nodded, shakily. It took nothing to put his nerves on edge.

He blew a breath. Closed his eyes and mumbled, "Dear, Lord, I don't know if You listening. G-ma said

You are so . . . yeah, You probably listening. Help me to do well. Amen."

He put his hand up and got a nod from Pee Wee, then began playing a beat that usually always got him a good 'nome score: *Boom tat boom tat tat. Boom tat boom tat tat. Tat tat tat tat tat tat tat tat . . . boom tat boom tat tat.*

Just as he was ready to get into it, Pee Wee's voice bassed, "Cool. We're good, Roland. Let's get it."

Rollie had no idea what that meant. He opened his mouth to ask when suddenly the audition song played overhead. His heart sped up. He'd rehearsed enough. Air drummed it enough and knew exactly when he was supposed to come in with the beat. Still, he missed his cue.

The music stopped.

"My bad," he said. Unsure if Pee Wee could hear him, he sat up straight and spoke louder. "My bad, I wasn't ready. But I am now."

"It's good," Pee Wee said, throwing a thumbs-up. "Take a breath, man. It's just me listening to how you vibe." When Rollie nodded understanding, he put up five fingers then slowly took away each one, counting down. He pointed at Rollie and the music played again.

This time, Rollie slid right in, caught the beat, and rode it.

His hands and feet were robots tapping out the sounds. He floated over his body and let them do their job.

SIMP

"Just remember to focus," Simp said. He took two steps away from behind Chrissy as Tai walked into the rec. Her, Bean, Mo, and Sheeda piled their thick coats on the small sofa, then crowded around the Ping-Pong table.

"You ready, girl?" Mo asked.

"I can't wait to see Chris wearing the sunflower costume," Sheeda said.

"I have to beat him first," Chrissy said. She swung gently at an invisible ball.

Simp looked toward the door. "Where Chris at? He backing out?"

At that moment, Simp wished for it. He didn't want to lose. The thought of having to dance in front of everybody at the rec had him in a panic like an angry fly trying to find its way out of a closed window. Chrissy had gotten better. But she played like she was scared. He couldn't do nothing about that. If he was Chris, he would slam the ball her way every time. It would be a sure win 'cause she'd be too busy flinching away from it. But she was dude's sister. He doubted Chris would come hard at her like that . . . if he showed up.

Just then Bean dashed his hopes.

"No, he's in the lobby talking to Roland," she said.

Simp stared at the door, fingers curling into a fist, waiting on them to walk in together. He stretched them straight, forcing himself not to care. He peeled his eyes away and listened to the girls talk.

"I'm ready for summer. I might be going to stay with my aunt," Sheeda said.

"Is anybody thinking about trying out for Sam Well's dance team?" Mo asked.

"Come on, Christol, you can do this," Bean said, with a light clap.

"Girl, I cannot with you and this wanting to call people by their whole name," Tai said, but she was already leaning into Bean in a halfway hug, laughing. It didn't seem to bother Bean, anyway. Simp had the feeling they weren't as tight as they had been before Tai's father got caught up on the molestation charges, but he had to give it to Bean—she rocked with Tai's teasing. He couldn't think of anybody she didn't get along with. For real, she was probably the reason Chrissy and Chris had melted into the squad so easily. Everything she did was about making everybody get along. It made him want to make things right with Rollie.

He pulled a stool over so he could coach Chrissy from the sidelines just as Chris walked through the door by his self. Simp waited for Rollie to walk in right behind him. When he didn't, Simp broke into a smile. His boy hadn't totally dipped on him.

Chris dropped his jacket onto the girls' pile. He pushed the sleeve of his T-shirt up and stood at the opposite end of the table, silent. Chris was one of the few dudes Simp knew that still rocked simple straight back cornrows. Most dudes in the Cove had locs, caesars, or twists. Chris wore his eight thick braids like he was still stuck back in whatever little boon he'd come from. Chris didn't seem to care what people thought about him. But he was gonna take an

L today if Simp had anything to do with it.

"Somebody got their game face on, I see," Simp yelled over at him.

Chris wouldn't take the bait.

"Where's Rollie, Chris?" Tai asked.

"I don't know," Chris said. He picked up his paddle. "You ready, Chrissy?"

"We gotta wait for Rollie," Tai said, neck stretching as she scanned the doorway.

Simp found himself watching, too. He'd been happy that Rollie hadn't rolled in with Chris, but now he wondered if Rollie was skipping out on watching. No matter what, they was never on the same page. Normally Simp would have texted him or walked out in the lobby to tell him to come on, but none of it felt right anymore. He wasn't gonna chase after him.

He scooted his stool so he was out of Chrissy's way but close enough to talk.

"You ready?" he said, with one last side glance toward the door.

She blew out a big breath. "Yeah. Let's go." She giggled. "It's stupid, but I'm nervous. Y'all please don't laugh if I lose."

"We won't," Bean promised.

"Girl, it's just your brother. And it's just us watching. You act like somebody taping it," Tai said.

"Eww, please, nobody post this. I'm serious," Chrissy said.

"Who gonna be the ref? Deontae can't do it 'cause he coaching," Chris said.

"I thought Rollie was gonna do it," Tai said, neck still craning on the lookout. "There he is. Rollie, come on, we ready start."

Simp wasn't sure whether the kick in his heart was fear or excitement. Then Rollie walked in and dapped him up without acknowledging Chris, and everything was good again. He was too relieved to talk trash.

"What's up, y'all?" Rollie asked, stuffing his hat into his coat pocket. He added to the coat pile and took his place at the side of the table. "Y'all ready?"

Chrissy and Chris nodded.

"You got this, C," Simp said.

Chrissy rolled her neck and nodded. "You serving, Chris?"

Chris tossed the ball her way. "Naw. You can serve first."

"And that's your doom, son. Come on, Chrissy, get that first point," Simp said, pumped.

He kept his eyes on Chris as Chrissy raised the ball. He could tell from the side of his eye that she had the ball too high, as usual. He clamped his mouth shut but cleared his throat. As if understanding, Chrissy lowered the ball and served. "Yes," he muttered under his breath.

They volleyed back and forth. That's what Chrissy had gotten best at. Simp prayed she could score. Chris wasn't into it at first, but as the ball kept coming back his way Simp saw the concentration in his eyes.

Simp leaned in, directing Chrissy with his mind.

"Try and score," he urged aloud.

Chrissy brought her hand back, smacked at the ball, and squealed when her brother missed. Everybody except Rollie clapped.

"Dang, Simp, let me find out you good at something. Got her all coached up," Mo said.

"Man, forget you, Mo," Simp said.

"Boy, I'm joking. Good job, Chrissy," Mo said.

"Point, Chrissy," Rollie said.

"So, nobody rooting for me?" Chris asked, smirking. "That's messed up about y'all."

"I'm with you, Chris," Bean said.

"Of course," Tai said with an eye roll.

"I still love you, Chrissy," Bean said, and made the heart sign with her hands.

"It's okay," Chrissy said, already bent in her serving stance.

"I mean, I'm not on anybody's side, for real," Tai said.

By the time the score was four to four, the cheers of the squad were so loud that everybody else in the rec had crowded around to see what was up.

Champ had started a side bet. A pile of quarters and dollar bills laid on the floor near Rollie's feet as Champ called out the newest bet—who would make the next point, whether the point was a slam, double bounce, or off the table.

In the Cove, if they could make bets on it, they did. It could be two roaches crawling up the wall. At some point somebody would spin a dollar out of their pocket onto the table or floor and say, "I bet that little sucker on the right get to the top first." And it was on.

Once money was involved, the game got heated. Mo became the official "can y'all shut up" assistant ref to help Rollie keep order.

Rollie put his hand up to quiet the arguing.

"Score goes to six. But you gotta win by two points,"

Rollie said, more to Chrissy than Chris.

"Wait, if I have five and he has six, does he win?" Chrissy asked.

"Naw, he gotta get seven then," Simp said. He could tell she didn't really get it.

Rollie waved the game to start again. The second the ball went up in the air, shouts of encouragement rang from everywhere. Thanks to the side bets, Chris had fans when they were betting on him. It gave him life and he scored fast.

"Game point," Rollie said, yelling above the cheers.

Simp shot up and was behind Chrissy. "Remember what I said. Watch his hands. He gonna try and slam you. Don't be scared. Slam back."

"Let her win on her own," Chris said, his face tight.

"She already owning you anyway," Simp said. He slid back onto the stool, his throat dry.

Chrissy swayed side to side. Her mouth was an O as she blew out in bursts. Simp was horrified as she closed her eyes just as Chris went to serve.

"He serving. He serving," he yelled, hopping up.

Chrissy's eyes popped open. She swung wild and it connected, sending the ball Chris's way. The ball double bounced.

"Chrissy's serve," Rollie said as groans from a new set of losing bettors rose.

"Oh my God, this is crazy," Sheeda said, hands over her eyes.

"We at least got to get the end on video," Tai said. She pulled her phone out and pointed it at the action. "Come on, Chrissy. You can do it."

Tai's video captured the rest. Caught when Chrissy pulled ahead to six. Saw Cappy yell, "Beat that trick, Chris." Which started an argument when Chris yelled back, "That's my sister, mark. Don't be calling her no trick." Zoomed in on Rollie keeping the peace as he made Cappy apologize.

The rec center buzzed with cheers and a few boos when Chrissy scored the winning point. Hands scrambled for their dollars. Some dissed Chris for losing. Others gave Chrissy her due for handling the game. Sheeda and Mo were hugging Chrissy in congratulations. Bean was standing by Chris, saying, "Good game." Seconds later he rigidly accepted a hug from his sister.

"Good game, but I ain't wearing no dance costume," Chris said.

"That was the bet," Chrissy said. Simp could tell by

her smile that she didn't take what he said that serious. She probably figured he was just saying it to save face and maybe he was, until Simp came over and asked, "What you say?"

"I said I'm not wearing no dance costume." Chris put his paddle down. He squared himself up to his tallest. "She won. I ain't taking that from her. But I ain't doing it."

Simp had expected Chris to do that. He wouldn't admit it to nobody, but if Chrissy had lost he would have done the same thing. Still, he wasn't about to let him just get away with reneging on the bet. All he'd meant to do was bark a little bit, so everybody saw that he was against Chris going back on his word. But it had got out of hand fast.

Later, Simp watched the video a dozen times. He didn't pay attention to nothing or nobody else except Rollie. The camera showed him in the same spot he'd stood while he ref'ed the game. Simp couldn't tell if he could hear what him and Chris was saying. It was a lot of noise. Even he had to put his ear to the phone to hear what him and Chris was saying. But it didn't matter. Rollie saw they was jawing at each other and never moved. Not even when Simp stepped in, inches from

Chris. Their faces close enough to feel each other's breath. Only the girls stopped them from fighting. Right before Simp went to swing, Bean and Chrissy pulled him back. Even Tai stopped taping and was up in the fray, keeping them apart.

The whole squad was between them, begging them to stop. Everybody but Rollie.

Simp watched it over and over.

Everybody but Rollie stepped in.

Everybody.

✳✳

ROLLIE

✳

G-ma pointed to a big black bag. Then a box. "Put those next to the door on your way out, please. Somebody from the church be by later to get 'em." She fanned herself.

Rollie had no idea why she was always hot. The heat felt like it was on five degrees. But her forehead was dotted with sweat. He grabbed the bag, toed the box with his foot, and headed for the stairs. Her voice stopped him. "I know it hurts, Ro, but it's not up to you to question God's will. He didn't want you in that band. He got something else in store for you."

His grandmother was always talking about God's

plan and how everything happened for a reason. Why would God want him hustling instead of in a real band? It didn't make sense. Rollie wasn't so sure He had as much control as G-ma thought. And he'd keep that to himself, for sure.

"Yes, ma'am," he said, hefting the bag in one hand, the box in the other.

His grandmother was on his heels as he balanced his way down the stairs. "Did Brother Monroe ever ask you about the Choral Review?"

"No, ma'am," Rollie said.

"He wanted to know if you could play for them. Brother Carl can't play that day. So, he was asking about you." Rollie heard the smile in her voice. "Now think about that. He want you cover for the regular drummer at the Choral Review. That service draw about two hundred people, Ro."

Rollie's eyes rolled. He was glad G-ma was behind him. He dropped the bag and box, careful not to slam it. G-ma detected any kind of attitude like it was her job.

"When is it?" he asked, scooting the junk out of the way of the door.

"Friday. Since your basketball games be on Saturday,

I told him you could do it," she said. "You can even ask some of your little friends to come. They having activities for the youth before the singing."

It took everything for Rollie not to go off. Why would she just say he could do it without asking him? He held his breath and counted to ten, waiting for the explosions in his head to die.

"My friends not trying sit in church on a Friday, G-ma," he said.

"Now how you know?" she asked, deadly serious.

Because I don't feel like being in church on Friday, Rollie wanted to yell. He knew better. And it wasn't G-ma he was mad at anyway. He didn't feel like drumming at all, definitely not for a Friday church event.

Whenever the youth choir got invited to do a special program, the services went on forever and his church always seemed like they got stuck as the last choir to perform. Not that it mattered. It wasn't like he could leave early if they went first. That's why he hated going.

Right now, drumming just reminded him he hadn't gotten the Rowdy Boys gig. He had barely gotten through TAG sessions that week. During 'nome drills he'd been behind the beat one day and ahead of it the next. No wonder the Rowdy Boys hadn't picked him. He sucked.

Worst, Mr. B kept trying to lift his spirits. Rollie appreciated it but he also wished he'd stop. Then when he got home, his mother started in asking was he all right. They acted like he was ready jump off a bridge or something. He just wanted everybody to stop talking about it. He tried out. He failed. It was over.

There was a knock at the door. He absently promised his grandmother he'd ask his friends about going to the Choral Review date, not meaning it, as he opened the door to Simp's face.

"What up?" Simp said, then immediately smiled when he heard G-ma ask who it was. He clicked on his manners. "How you doing, Ms. Matthews?"

"Deontae, come on in. You haven't been around in a long time," G-ma said, her arms opened for a hug. "Where you been?"

Simp walked into the embrace then quickly stepped back as if embarrassed by the affection. "I usually have to watch my brothers or I'm at practice. So—"

G-ma was ready to start with the "how's your mother" line when Rollie grabbed his duffel bag and turned foot to the door. "All right, we heading to practice," he said.

"Is your homework done?" G-ma asked.

Rollie was already outside, willing to risk the wrath he'd catch later. Simp said a hasty good-bye and was right behind him.

Only a handful of kids were outside in the darkening evening. They made enough noise for a gang of people.

Three boys ran past them, racing in the street. One of them had taken his jacket off, in the cold, and was blowing past the other two, his head up, arms pumping.

'Rauders material, Rollie thought bitterly.

"You good?" Simp asked, when the boys had flown past them.

"Yup," Rollie said.

"Can I holler at you for a second?" Simp asked.

"Long as it don't make us late. You know how Tez is," Rollie said.

If Simp caught his sarcasm, he didn't let on.

"If I came off wrong last weekend when I asked you if you dimed us out to Chris, that's my bad," he said. "I mean it. I wasn't trying say you was a rat."

"It's swazy," Rollie said.

"Naw, but it ain't swazy between us, Rollie." Simp looked toward the rec like he was gauging how much time they had. He stopped walking. "I came off wrong.

I'm coming at you admitting that. But if things between us was good, why ain't you jump in the other day when me and Chris almost got scrapping?"

"You serious, right now?" Rollie asked.

"Yeah, I am," Simp said. "I keep coming to you man to man about stuff and it's like you playing me."

Rollie's lips screwed to the left. He bit the bottom of his lip thinking. All he wanted to do was get to practice. Ball. Go home. He started to say that then walk away, but Simp pushed it by adding, "You ain't being real, son."

Anger blossomed in his belly, making it work for Rollie to keep his voice under control. "Why? 'Cause I don't feel like being your shadow while you big man on the court?"

Simp frowned. "It don't gotta be all that. I—"

"Son, look," Rollie said, raising his voice before lowering it to normal. "Whatever beef you got with Chris ain't my beef, Simp. Period. That's all and that's it."

Simp's eyes were bugging out of his head. "So, if we had got into it you was just gon' stand there and watch?"

"It didn't get to all that, though," Rollie said.

"But if it had?" Simp said, challenging.

"I ain't even going there, yo," Rollie said, walking again.

Simp was at his side in an instant. "'Rauders ride or die. How you not gonna have my back? Even Cappy 'nem was ready jump in."

"That's Cappy 'nem. You and Chris was ready brawl over a Ping-Pong game. I wasn't wit' it," Rollie snapped.

"Oh, so now we only got each other back if it's over certain stuff?" Simp's voice was high-pitched and unbelieving.

"Whatever, man," Rollie said, done with the conversation. Done with everything.

Simp grabbed his shoulder, pulling him around. "It's like that?"

Rollie resisted the urge to swing.

They were stopped in front of the rec center. Some of their teammates were inside the lobby, joking around with some girls. For once, Rollie didn't want anything more than to be in practice, not talking, not thinking. He couldn't keep doing this. Not with Simp. Not with Chris. Not with anybody.

"Is it like what?" he asked.

"You gonna pick and choose when you have my back?" Simp said.

"If that's what you want believe," Rollie said.

He stayed staring into the rec's lobby as Simp went on talking loyalty.

Rollie knew he was wrong. He should have jumped in. But everything had popped off too fast. Cappy didn't even know what the ruckus was about and he'd been ready to jump in. If he had, it would have been bad. The rest of the team would have done the same. Chris was wrong for reneging, no doubt, but it was a Ping-Pong game. It wasn't worth stomping him for. He wanted to say all that to Simp.

There wasn't any point, though. Holding up for somebody going back on a bet was up there with snitching. It wasn't done. No matter what he said, he'd be wrong.

Simp's locs shook and shivered around his face as his voice rose. "All I got is what I saw, Rollie. You ain't try jump in. Is that how me and you rock now?"

"I left it between y'all to handle," Rollie said, refusing to raise his voice.

"That's a punk move," Simp said.

The slow ticktock of Simp's head, like he was a

father disappointed in his son, angered Rollie.

"All right then, I'm a punk," he snapped. Simp's mouth opened and closed without sound. Rollie put his hands up in surrender. "So, I'm good off that."

There was hurt in Simp's eyes, but his words were bitter. "Naw, I know you good. You always good, right?" He took a step back like he'd catch Rollie's rattiness if he stood too close. His chin stiffened. "And, like you said, I woulda handled Chris if it came to that. I ain't need you."

Everything in Rollie wanted to stop before it came to blows. But he couldn't stand down.

"Good, 'cause I can't always be babysitting you or the team. I got stuff going on."

"Then maybe you got too much going on," Simp said.

Yeah, thanks to you, Rollie thought bitterly. He clamped his teeth down hard on his tongue to stop himself. Simp was the one that got them caught up in this whole mess in the first place, but now it was somehow on Rollie that he couldn't handle it all?

The silvery taste of blood dotted his tongue. His hands itched to punch Simp in the face. His eyes slid over to the glass, watching their friends talk, unaware

PAULA CHASE

their two best players were ready to get into it. If they got to fighting would anybody be on his side? He doubted it. It deflated him.

"Yup. I do got a lot going on. We done?" he asked, his face blank. "I wouldn't want to be late and have to do sprint drills."

He walked past his teammates and sat in the gym alone. Anger and loneliness made his face hot the way it did when the only thing that could cool it down was tears. He gulped them back. Stamped the loneliness away and let the anger simmer.

Later that night, still stewing in bitterness, he made a new group chat with everybody in it except Simp: *y'all can joke me later all u want but I promised my grandmother I would ask if anybody want come to Mt. Ezekial's choral review. So I asked.* 💀

Embarrassment and shame crept up his neck. He didn't really even want his friends to see him playing gospel music. But a part of him wanted to get at Simp. Show which one of them had the squad's love.

He guessed he had their love.

Slowly they buzzed in. One message. Two. Five. He didn't pick up the phone and look until he'd counted twelve messages.

She-da-Man: *Ayyy I'm praise dancing at the review. So I'll be there* 😀

JahMeeLah: *Is this the same thing you dancing in Sheeda?*

JahMeeLah: *Oops just saw ur message.*😀 *I'll be there already @Roll-Oh gotta be there for my girl* 😉

Chriss-E: *We not doing anything. I wanna hang.*

Yo'MChris: *Church? Friday night? I think I hear my mother calling me* 🏃

Mo'Betta: *He wrong.*😀 *I be there too.*

DatGirlTai: 👀 *How ya'll getting there doe?*

Mo'Betta: *Umm when Sheeda asked u earlier u said u couldn't go.* 🤔 *pressed now that Rollie asked u to go?* 😂

DatGirlTai: *W/e Mo. I couldn't go at first. But 4 Yo Information H3 rehearsal got cancelled that night.* 🙄

Mo'Betta: *Sure you couldn't.*

She-da-Man: *Wait . . . why Simp not in this chat?* 👀

DatGirlTai: *For real Sheeda? Obvs Rollie didn't put him in dis chat. And bt-dubs y'all got too many chats.* 😠 *I'm ready start getting 'em mixed up. Don't even say nothing Mo.* 🙄

Mo'Betta: *Simp probably not trying be in church anyway fr fr*

Rollie pushed through the guilt stabbing at him for

leaving Simp out. It was done now so . . .

Roll-Oh: *y'all just made my g-ma very happy* 😛

A barrage of messages hit the chat as the squad dog piled, teasing him for being pressed for them to attend. He took the jokes in stride, happy but a little nervous about the squad seeing him play at church.

SIMP

Simp sat on the front stoop of the row. It was like sitting on a block of ice. He zipped up his Angel-approved puffy jacket, burying his head into its hood, and sunk his hands into the pockets, willing the little bit of warmth to travel to his legs. Part of him wanted to go back inside where it was warm. Where he was in control. At least usually he was in control.

His brothers were too restless today. He couldn't keep fussing. He needed some air or space. Or both.

Things between him and Rollie hadn't gone nothing how he had wanted. He hadn't even came off wrong and still Rollie shaded him, not even giving Simp a chance to let him know that in the end he was just hurt. They went too far back for all this beefing. But he didn't know how to make it right no more. And Rollie didn't seem like he cared if they did. Except in practice, they were barely talking to each other.

As long as they'd been friends they had lived by the same code—having each other's back wasn't nothing new. Simp didn't understand why it was changing. No music program, not even some new kid should have changed that.

He wanted to stay mad that Rollie hadn't jumped in. He couldn't, though.

Rollie was the only friend he had who would understand how he was feeling about keeping Dre out the game. And Simp hadn't been able to say nothing about it because either the squad was around or things were blowing up between them.

On top of that, the more he had to be out for 'Rauders business, the worst things got with Dre.

He was sitting out in the cold waiting on Angel instead of inside the house because the second he told Dre he had to make a run, his brother's eyes had gone dead. He sat in that corner chair, mouth clamped tight, staring through the TV. Simp wanted to blow up on him, tell him soldier up and deal with it. But he didn't have the heart, this time.

If Dre had a buddy he could call and chop it up with, it would be different. Maybe a lot of things would be.

As the cold froze his skin, Simp wondered if Dre would care about playing for the Marauders if he could be outside ripping and running with his own friends who played for the Cougars. Simp remembered when Dre used to want to play for them, but somebody had to be home when Simp wasn't. After a while, Dre had convinced himself that the rec league was for scrubs. He made peace with getting to middle school, knowing it meant he could be like Simp and hoop with the 'Rauders.

First, Simp was cool with it. Who wouldn't want their little brother to want to be like them?

He shuddered.

He didn't want Dre to be like him no more.

By the time Angel pulled up, his Civic purring like a tiger, Simp was frozen in place. The car's heat, still blowing cold, attacked his face. He wiggled in the car's seat, trying to get blood to return to his thighs.

He watched the scenery change from strip malls

and bus stops to wooded communities with names like Ridge on the Bay as they drove the six short miles out of the hood and over the DRB Bridge. They got silent permission from the big houses standing guard. Once they were over the bridge, the trees surrounding the houses seemed to give him and Angel cover.

When Angel had hit him up, letting him know about the next run, Simp hadn't slept that night. He was ready this time. Ready to be Angel's eyes. His ears. Whatever he needed. He had to learn the game in and out.

Low-key, he was nervous. Angel was probably going to make him pump the gas soon. What if he messed it up?

He sat back in the seat, his eyes probing the road ahead of them, waiting for the first stop. He didn't realize he was blowing his breath out, hyping himself up, until Angel asked, "You good?"

Simp felt Angel's eyes on the side of his face. He soldiered up by slumping in the seat, like he was just cooling out.

"All day," he said. He was nervous and that was bad enough. But his mind wasn't clear, and Angel asking was he good made everything weigh on him heavier.

Dre's future.

Him and Rollie not talking.

And even though it felt stupid that he cared—the squad hadn't hung out since the Ping-Pong game. He had a feeling maybe they had and just hadn't told him. He sunk down farther in the seat, depressed at the thought they were icing him and mad that it mattered.

Angel knocked him on the shoulder. "I told Unc you be ready soon."

Simp glanced over, felt his eyes get big, and narrowed them. "To pump the gas?"

Angel's laugh was easy. "Yeah."

Simp looked straight ahead as Angel started the day's lesson. "Hardest part is looking like you ain't doing nothing." He cranked the radio up, nodding to the beat, and raised his voice over the music. "These White boys over here love partying. Shoot, I be running out of gas stations to hit soon."

"You scared of getting caught?" Simp asked. Angel was sixteen, not old enough to be put in the clink, but Simp had heard plenty stories about Boys Town—the juvenile center—he didn't want end up there, either.

"Not no more. Far as anybody know, me and these dudes just ran into each other and chopping it up." He shrugged. "You do it right, that's all anybody gonna think." He eyed Simp head to toe. "Before I let you do it, we got get you hooked up, though. Hoodies and locs hiding your face be making people pay attention to you." He laughed. "They assume you ready jack 'em or something."

Simp touched his thick hair. "I got cut 'em?" A slice of panic went down his heart.

"Naw. But probably put 'em up or something. Or wear a band so they held back," Angel said. "Just sayin,' you got look more like somebody one of these White dudes might really know from school or whatever. That's all."

Simp soaked it in. He stayed rocking T's, hoodies, and boots. Angel was always clean looking like he went to private school or something with polos, jeans, and super icy sneaks—never ever a blemish on his shoes. He couldn't see his self going school like that, but he'd do it for the run.

"My uncle think you the next one up. I can see that. I was like you when I was thirteen," Angel said.

Pride pushed Simp up straighter in the seat. All he'd wanted, at first, was to head a small crew, but if Coach Tez thought he could work solo, he could be down with that. If he did it right, Coach wouldn't need Dre.

"Having a crew is cool. But I ain't really kick it with nobody but Raheem. Heem was never 'bout the game, though," Angel said. "Since Unc ain't send your boy, Rollie, with us—you ready be put on by yourself?"

"No doubt," Simp said.

"How your boy gonna feel about it?" Angel asked.

Simp opened his mouth, ready to assure Angel that Rollie was still down for whatever.

"Rollie probably be all right with it," Simp said instead. "He got other stuff going on. He into music and whatnot."

"Yeah, that's how Heem was with basketball. His hustle was the court. When my uncle asked him about running for him, Heem said no."

"He ain't never run? Even when he played for the 'Rauders?" Simp asked, squinting to hide his shock.

"Nah. That just wasn't him. The game ain't for everybody. Know what I'm saying?" Angel said.

"Yeah," Simp said, stuck on somebody telling Tez no. He wanted a minute to think about what that meant, but the car was pulling into the gas station.

He shut his mind off and turned the light on in his eyes to scope out the new station. It only had two pumps. A dude with red hair and a DRB High wrestling jacket was walking away from the window, where the attendant was already back to reading a magazine. Red-haired dude's car was already at the pump. He walked over and began pumping gas.

Angel slid out the car.

Simp heard a low "What up?" before the closing door shut out the rest. He sat back in the seat, face forward, watching but not watching as Angel played the game.

ROLLIE

Mr. B's hand shot up. The music stopped like somebody had pulled a plug. He scratched his head, eyes wandering from the lead vocalist, to the keyboard player, then bass player, to Rollie. "The magic not gonna happen today." He lifted his hands in an unasked question. "Y'all not hitting it. It's okay. Some days you're the drummer. And some days you're the drum. So, let's go ahead and quit a little early."

Not a single person argued. There were muttered good-byes as everyone packed away their equipment. Days like this, Rollie was glad to be the drummer. All he had to do was get up and go.

He stuffed his drumsticks in his bag and was halfway to the door when Mr. B called his name.

Please don't talk about the audition again, Rollie thought.

"Yes, sir," he said.

"You have my permission," Mr. B said. He stood watch over Rollie, his arms folded.

"Permission for what?" Rollie asked.

Mr. B's brown face broke into a big smile. He sat on the desk's corner. "To be over it, Roland. One audition not even close to the end of the world if you really want to do this music thing one day." He put his hand up. "*If* you want to do it. And that's a big *if*. You're thirteen. Maybe today you want to be a drummer. Next month you might want be in the NBA. And next year you might want to be an engineer. I'm giving you permission to want to be all that. To want to pursue all that. To dream far and wide and stop worrying about the outcome of one single day."

"Yes, sir," Rollie said. A wave of anger crashed in on his head then eased out. It left him sad for a second, and then he felt relief. His face burned. He was going to cry, right here in front of Mr. B. He balled his hands into fists and swallowed hard to push back the spit growing in his mouth.

Mr. B hopped up and hurried the last straggling student along. "All right, Kerry, see you Friday. Bring that voice I like."

Kerry pepped up as she waved and sang good-bye. Mr. B shut the door behind her and was back at his spot on the desk as a tear slid down Rollie's face.

He sniffed to keep the others back, but they leaked just the same. He swiped at the tears. He wasn't sure why he was crying. All he knew was he couldn't stop.

Mr. B pulled a tissue out of the box on the desk and handed it to him. He waited until Rollie got the tears under control—like students stood crying in his classroom every day.

Mr. B clasped his hands softly in front of him. "That's good. 'Cause now you just gave yourself permission. I think you can move on and start enjoying TAG sessions again."

Rollie's mouth opened to object, but Mr. B was right. He'd been miserable the last two weeks. He didn't want to be. He just hadn't known how to stop.

"Friday, come in ready to enjoy music again. Deal?"

Rollie shook Mr. B's outstretched hand. He felt lighter when he left the music room. He thought about stopping by the bathroom to see if his eyes were red. He couldn't do anything about it if they were. The squad was gonna have a good time with that.

As he hit the straightaway leading to the lobby he saw them, already gathered, and realized he was glad whether he got teased or not. He needed the comfort of the squad's constant chatter.

He sidled up to their circle and it opened enough for him to fit in between Chris and Mila.

"What up?" Chris said, fist out.

Rollie tapped it with his own. "Everybody get out early today?"

"We always do in dance so we have time to get dressed," Mo said.

"Ms. Suitor was sick and ain't nobody tell me I didn't have drama today," Sheeda said, openly annoyed.

"Umm, she was the only one who showed up, though," Chrissy said, with a sly smile.

Mo held up a single finger. "Out of thirty people she was the lonely only."

"I been sitting out here in the lobby looking like Boo-Boo the fool," Sheeda said, shaking her head.

Everybody jumped in on the joke and Sheeda took it like a champ. She could be like a puppy trying to find somebody willing to pick them up. She was easy to tease, and Mo was usually the hardest on her. But let anybody else get on Sheeda too much and Mo stepped right in. Rollie didn't get how it was okay for Mo to go in on her. It was one of those things he left alone. The girls had more rules than he could keep up with.

"What up, Rollie and crew?"

The circle parted as they all turned toward Zahveay. He tapped Rollie's fist with his own, but stayed outside the circle, unwilling to close the gap. Rollie started to let him know Simp wasn't around, but a part of him liked that Zah respected that he wasn't really part of the squad. Simp was too hard on dude.

Mo frowned. "Unah, no you not gonna act like we don't have our own names, Zahveay."

Zah smiled sheepishly. "My bad, Monique."

She rolled her eyes but smiled. "That's what I thought."

"I heard you in TAG now," Sheeda said.

A huge grin burst across Zahveay's face. "Yup. Today was my first session."

"Ay, so which program you in?" Rollie asked.

"Dance," Mo and Mila sang.

"Oh, for real?" Rollie squinted. "No shade, but you do ballet and stuff?"

"Naw. I tap dance," Zahveay said. He looked from Rollie to Chris, uneasily. When they didn't joke him, he happily went on. "I been tap dancing since third grade."

"How come you didn't try out last summer?" Chrissy asked.

"Exactly. How you get in without auditioning?" Mo asked, salty. "Everybody went through two days all nervous and having to stand in front of judges and now you just in it?"

Zahveay shrugged.

"I mean, you know somebody or something?" Mo asked, insistent.

"Maybe it's because he's really good," Mila said, nudging Mo with her shoulder.

"Or, maybe he just don't want y'all all up in his sauce," Chris said.

He and Rollie snickered.

"I heard it's 'cause it's only, like, one other boy in the program and they wanted more," Sheeda said, peering at Zah for confirmation.

Mo scowled. "Wait, that's wrong. They made all the girls try out? But just 'cause they want boys he get to walk up into this?" She looked Zahveay up and down. "You better be good, too."

Rollie took pity on him by changing the subject.

"Everybody coming to the 'Peake?"

The chorus of "yes" echoed in the big empty lobby. Zahveay sent him a silent thank you with his eyes. He stayed just outside the circle, piping in where he could. Rollie relaxed into details about who would ride with who to the game. Who was going out for pizza afterward. Whether the 'Rauders could do the impossible and hold on to state champs for a sixth time in a row. Zahveay smartly stayed quiet.

Rollie fed off his friends' excitement. Nothing brought the hood together like the 'Rauders winning the 'Peake. There'd be a big celebration at the rec with food and music. People would treat the team like celebrities for weeks after. Everything felt possible when they won. They could definitely do it again as long as him and Simp were vibing.

Right now they still were—on the court—and that was going to have to do for now.

Rollie was high on the confidence. Once the bus dropped them home, he jogged from the bus stop straight to practice. Champ greeted him at the door. "What up, Rollie?"

They exchanged a hand grip. "Ain't nothing," Rollie said.

"Man, I lost twenty dollars on your boy's Ping-Pong game," Champ said.

"Ain't nobody tell you take bets," Rollie said, making sure to keep his voice joking.

Champ's laughter echoed as they entered the gym. "Yo, ain't no way I thought lil' mama was gonna beat him, though. I was like, winning this money gonna be easier than hitting a lick." He put his hand to his mouth and announced his entrance with a loud "Cooty-hoooo."

The return call echoed through the gym. Rollie scanned the room. Simp wasn't there yet. His absence didn't mean to wait to start. If they goofed off until the captain or coach showed up, they got extra drills.

Rollie dropped his bag and headed to the line behind the basket, the signal to start warm ups—two jogs up and down the full length of the court, then three all-out sprints the same distance. Midway across the floor, Simp came in with Cappy. They were laughing over something and dapping each other up. Rollie picked up his speed to outrun the jealousy creeping into his chest. He watched them from the side of his eye.

Dre trailed behind them. Cappy handed Dre his bag and jacket.

"Why y'all punks ain't lined up for the press?" Cappy yelled to stragglers as he took his own time getting in place.

Everyone jogged their way over. Once someone reached the line, they instinctively began an easy run down to the other end. The team trickled down the gym until just about everybody was in motion, either starting or heading back.

Rollie paced himself down the court to get the blood flowing and slyly watched Simp and his brother. Simp was on the bleacher, taking his time gathering his locs into two gigantic-sized Princess Leia buns. As he tucked the hair into whatever band was holding it all together, he looked up at Dre—who was still holding Cappy's stuff—and sternly imparted some kind of advice. Dre's back was to the court, but his head bobbed in a steady nod.

By the time Rollie headed down the court for his first sprint, Simp and Dre were in the mix, jogging. Simp's stride was long. Dre easily kept up with his taller brother.

"Captain on the line," Cappy yelled.

Everyone picked up their pace. If Simp finished before somebody who had already started, everybody would do extra drills.

The team flowed seamlessly up and down the line then peeled off to stretch.

Simp joined them on the sideline. He talked smoothly through his heaving chest.

"Y'all all know my knucklehead brother Dre, right?"

"What up, D?" Champ yelled, his fist raised.

Dre lifted his head in a nod before going to the floor and duplicating Cappy's hamstring stretch.

"Dre working out with us today, trying see if he can hang," Simp said.

"Fresh meat," Reuben said, rubbing his hands together.

"Bruh, he just working out with us," Cappy said, eyeing Simp for approval.

"And what?" Reuben scowled. "We gon' take it easy on him? Pssh, naw, he finna get worked out."

Dre's eyes skittered from Reuben to Cappy. If Simp felt sorry for what Dre was in for, it didn't show on his face. Rollie's eyebrow twitched in surprise as Simp said, "Rollie, he gon' take your place on point today."

He was grateful when Champ spoke up. "You

putting in a scrub while we trying get ready for the 'Peake?"

"Ay, yo, if you got a problem with it, Coach be here in a hot minute," Simp said, unsmiling.

Champ put his hands up in surrender. "I ain't say I had a problem."

"It's cool," Rollie said, his throat tight.

No one else seemed bothered. They weren't the ones being replaced. One by one they got up and took their places on the court before Tez walked in.

Rollie pushed himself up off the floor as cobwebs of worry weaved into his thoughts. Dre could take his place next season—no doubt. On the court, he was an angry hornet buzzing around you protecting its nest.

Rollie was torn.

If the team would still be good, maybe Tez wouldn't care whether Rollie came back next season. Still, the back of Rollie's neck tingled. Nobody ever worked out with the team unless they were on the team. Or, connected to the team.

When Simp stood up, Rollie pulled him in for a grip and when his ear was close enough he asked, "Dre know what's up?"

"All day," Simp said. He barked at his brother. "Let's

go. Youn want still be stretching when Coach walk in."

Rollie lagged behind as they walked to the court, feeling dissed.

Whenever he made the mistake of forgetting basketball wasn't ever just basketball with the Marauders, the reality jabbed him in the face. He'd been excited for practice today. Had been up for it, until he remembered that.

The bounce of the ball pounded Simp's words into his head.

All day.

Dre knew what he was getting into and Simp was letting him.

SIMP

Finally, everything was going his way. The 'Rauders were looking good in practice. Angel was hinting that he might let Simp get a third run. And, for some reason, Tai was blowing up his phone.

It wasn't that he was trying get with Tai—he knew she was checking for Rollie, but what was he gonna do, tell her not to text him?

He kept one eye on the phone and the other on the TV screen where Dom was out-balling Cappy's team by twenty points and it was only halftime. Dom couldn't do that on a real court, but watching Cappy's team get manhandled made Simp proud of his nerdy little brother.

He rolled his eyes at Tai's message:

y u ain't tell me Rollie auditioned for TRB?

He didn't know what she was talking about. Sometimes Tai could be hella nosy. She acted like people was supposed to report to her on every little thing they did. He hit her back quick with—*TRB who dat?*—just as Dom made a big move.

"Ohhh son, he broke your ankle," Simp screamed at Cappy. He tapped Dom in the back of the head. "You got him on the run."

Cappy's hands moved frantically over the controller. "Yo, how he even do that?"

"Family secret," Simp said.

Dre bounced on his toes near Dom, egging him on. "Yuh. Yuh. We ball hard."

"Man, y'all messing up my concentration," Cappy said, elbowing Dre away.

Simp drowned out Cappy's whining as he reread Tai's message.

DatGirlTai: *Hello, The Rowdy Boys! The go-go band.* 🥁

GreatEight: *Where u hear dat at? Rumors be wild*

DatGirlTai: *not a rumor.* 😼 *Rollie told me hisself cuz I asked y was he being so salty all the time. I felt bad when he said he ain't make da band.* 😕 *So u ain't know either?*

A low buzz started in the back of Simp's head and made its way to the front as he put things together. That was the audition Rollie's moms had mentioned? The frickin' Rowdy Boys?

DatGirlTai: *I told Rollie he was wrong for not telling nobody. U know how he is tho.* 😠

DatGirlTai: *but for real I figured u knew.*

GreatEight: *he told me he had a audition*

DatGirlTai: *and u ain't say nothing?!?!* 😠 🤭 *that's messed up about y'all. How u gon keep that from the squad? It's the ROWDY BOYS!*

GreatEight: *how I look spreading his bizness?*

DatGirlTai: *whatever Simp. I'm bout to cut both y'all off.*

GreatEight: *do what u gotta do, shawty*

He put the phone down, ignoring its noise as Tai's messages, likely fussing him out, buzzed in. The living room roared with noise as Dre celebrated Dom's win.

"You played yourself," Dre said. "For real, he did the same move on you three times." He shoved his fingers in Cappy's face. "Three, son. Three."

Cappy smacked Dre's hands out his face. "Go 'head, yo."

"Can I play him next?" Derek asked, tugging on Dre's T-shirt.

"Here," Dom said, handing Derek the controller.

"Come on, Cappy. It's my turn," Derek said, giddy.

Cappy pleaded with Simp. "Ay, yo, get your brothers. They wylin'."

Simp let the chaos build a few more minutes. Derek and Dre yapped at Cappy, taunting him. Dom was the only one who took the win in stride, sitting quiet on the sofa beside Simp, content to let things play out. When Cappy's face turned to stone, Simp stepped in.

"All right, all right. Y'all need to chill," he said, not bothering to raise his voice.

Derek shut it down, quick.

Dre kept up the muttering. "If you can't take the beatdown, don't step in the ring."

Simp stared him down until he dropped, sullen, into the corner chair.

"We still playing?" Derek asked.

"Naw, I'm out," Cappy said, angling his controller toward Dre.

Dre mean-mugged, refusing to take it. Cappy shrugged and laid it in the folding chair where he'd been sitting.

"Nobody want play me?" Derek whined.

"I play you," Dom said, hopping up.

"I wanted to play Cappy, though," Derek said.

"He already said he ain't want play. Stop crying like a little girl," Simp said.

Derek pouted. "I ain't crying."

"Then play Dom or turn the game off," Simp said.

Derek sat, shoulders sagging, facing the TV. Dom slid into place next to their little brother, anxious to keep the peace. "Come on, Stink. You can pick your team first."

Derek brightened. "I want be the Lakers."

"Dre, go check on Little Dee," Simp said.

"We can hear him on the monitor," Dre said, scowling.

Simp didn't have to ask twice. Dre stalked up the stairs. When he came back he sulked in the corner away from the action of the more quiet game between his younger brothers. Simp played a game on his phone. He had three messages from Tai. He didn't look at them. Cappy sat on the other end of the couch, the beatdown already forgotten. He pulled his phone out, grinned, and shone the screen in Simp's direction.

"Ay, yo, Mo just hit me up."

Simp snorted. "For what?"

"That's my bidness," Cappy said, showing every tooth in his mouth with his smile.

Simp didn't bother to bust his bubble. Mo didn't check for dudes like him and Cappy. Mo was boughetto—half bougie but more ghetto. She was the only girl in a house of three brothers and never had a problem putting you in your place. She never let nobody talk bad about her brothers being in and out of jail, but something about her made it clear she was trying be above their thuggery. He couldn't see her ever paying attention to Cappy.

His dark chocolate skin stayed so ashy, the team had once gave him a lotion bottle labeled Cappy Cream. It was probably still somewhere under the bleachers where Cappy had kicked it. His eyes were like two dark marbles set real far back in his face. His fade stood nearly half a foot high off his head. He said he was trying grow locs, but Simp figured he just liked how his hair made him taller.

Like Simp, Cappy was thirteen but only in seventh grade. Dude could be annoying, but it was never no doubt he had your back in the streets or on the court, and when the rest of the squad moved on he'd be all Simp had.

Simp caught himself. It was the first time he had thought about Rollie leaving the team without a streak of panic zipping down his chest. If Rollie was on the come up enough to try out for TRB, it was gonna happen sooner or later anyway, wasn't it?

It wasn't none of his business. He had his own problems.

Instead, he taunted Cappy's grinning face.

"I can't even see Mo messing with no hood dude, for real," he said.

Cappy's eyes disappeared as his face crinkled in confusion. "She from the hood, how she not gon' mess with no hood dude?"

Simp hesitated. Everybody was changing, these days. Maybe Mo would let Cappy get at her. He played it off, trying to change the subject. "Don't even worry 'bout it. You know how Tez feel about females—" He lowered his voice imitating their coach. "If you out here chasing the cat, you ain't chasing the cash."

"Yo, you sound just like him." Cappy laughed and put his fist out for dap. "But, for real, Coach Tez got, like, three girlfriends. How he gon' talk?"

"I bet you won't ask him that," Simp said. He sneered at Cappy's openmouthed silence. "That's what

I thought. I don't know about you, but right now I'm about chasing that cash."

"Word to that," Cappy said.

They slapped hands twice then slid the hand down the side of their head.

The door swung open, crashing against the wall. Cappy jumped up, fists clenched. Niqa Wright walked in, arm full of grocery bags, fussing.

"Why ain't nobody answer my damned text? I told you I would be here in ten minutes and to meet me at the door to get these bags."

Simp and his brothers grabbed the bags.

Cappy's eyes darted past their mother like he expected trouble behind her.

"How you doing, Kevin? Your arms broken? You can't grab a bag?" Niqa said.

Cappy grabbed the last bag. "Sorry, Ms. Niqa."

She sat down on a small love seat, her seat and the cleanest piece of furniture in the house. "I tell you what, I'm about to strip phones away if y'all not gonna answer me."

"Ma, can I have whoever phone you take?" Derek asked.

Niqa threw darts, with her eyes, at her two older

sons. "Um-huh. You sure can, baby."

"We ain't see your text, Ma. We was into the game," Simp said, praying she would let it be. He didn't want Cappy to see them get into it. He was grateful when she kicked her shoes off and directed her anger elsewhere.

"These damned shoes cute but they hurt my feet. Derek, bring me those canned green beans," she said.

He was up and back with the can in seconds. "Can we finish playing, Ma?"

She waved him off, the closest thing to a yes she ever gave when she was settling into a bad mood. She sat the can on the floor and rubbed her feet over it as she complained about the living room being a mess.

"Ay, Ma, Dre worked out with the team the other day," Simp said. He was relieved when his mother's head lifted in curiosity. "Dre did real good. Tez already calling him Pitbull."

"Ma, I was balling my tail off," Dre said. He came and sat on the arm of the love seat.

Niqa shoved him off. "Boy get your butt off my sofa," she said, then just as quickly praised him. "You did good, huh? That's good, Boo."

"Coach Martinez said I'm the one to watch at tryouts," Dre said, beaming.

Their mother sucked her teeth. "Tryouts? He saw what you got, what you need try out for?"

"Everybody got try out," Simp said.

"First of all, watch how you talk to me." Her finger stayed pointed in Simp's direction a second longer than necessary. "Second, that raggedy team need my boys. Martinez better recognize." She opened her arms. "Give me a hug, Dre Dre. You know you got this. Them tryouts for the wannabes that show up thinking they can ball. You as good as on the team. Ain't he, Deontae?"

Simp's jaw worked. Why his mother have to say all that in front of Cappy? If Cappy went back and told anybody that Dre ain't need try out . . .

But just as quickly as his mother had started it, she pushed herself up, sending the can rolling across the floor toward the kitchen. It clunked against the dirty tile floor before thudding quietly against the wall.

"I bought the groceries. Somebody else can cook 'em," she said, before heading up the stairs. Dre followed her, asking if he could get new basketball shoes. Her reply, more rant than answer, was lost as they disappeared upstairs.

Cappy found his voice the second she left. "That's cool how your moms want Dre be on the team. My mother been wanting me to quit. She act like 'Rauders is why I be failing." His shoulders straightened. "But it ain't. School be hard."

Simp could only nod. Everything except math and PE bored him. He had gave up trying to explain to his mother and the guidance counselor that no matter what he did, he couldn't keep up with how fast everything moved. The class would be halfway through a book and he'd still be on the second chapter. They'd cover a chapter in another class and be expected to take a quiz on it the next day. He didn't understand how everybody moved so fast. And if he asked, they would think he was stupid. So he left it alone, did what he could, and hoped it was enough. When it wasn't, it wasn't.

"My mother told me if I failed again, then basketball a wrap," Cappy said.

Simp laughed, hard. "Shoot, mines probably make me knuckle up if I ever tried to quit the team."

"My moms don't like Coach Martinez." Cappy's voice lowered, forcing Simp to lean in to hear over his brothers' growing trash talking. "She know about the side hustle." His eyes pointed upward toward the stairs. "Your moms know?"

Simp wouldn't say it aloud, but him and Cappy exchanged a knowing look.

"Man, one day she made me go to his house with her. And she laid him out. Like, for real cussed him out. I was scared he was gon' pull out a heater on my moms, son." Cappy's head shook side to side at the memory. "Told him it was disgusting that he was using basketball to sell drugs. And laid into him about how he the reason our hood always the first community they name when they talking about crime."

Simp's heart raced like he was reliving it with Cappy. "Tez ain't do nothing?" he asked.

"You know how he do. He kept calling her ma'am and saying she had it all wrong." Cappy chuckled. "For a minute even I believed him. But then she asked him was he using me to hustle. He looked her dead in the eye and said no. So, she asked me was I doing it—" He shuddered, blinked himself out of the memory, then shrugged. "And I lied too. Said I wasn't."

"And she believed you?" Simp asked.

"For real, I don't know. But she told him I better only be playing basketball or she would call the cops herself on him and me. Ain't that wild? Calling po-po on her own son." Cappy's eyes shifted to the game away from Simp's gaze as he cleared his throat. "I figured Tez wouldn't put me on the road anymore after that. But he put me out there when he know she at work, and he find other stuff for me to do so she don't catch me." He eyed the stairs. "You lucky, though. Your moms know and she down with it. Shoot, if Dre get put on to the hustle, y'all gonna be icy with cash."

It didn't feel like luck to Simp.

ROLLIE

Lunchtime was the kind of chaos Rollie liked. The babbling of two hundred eighth graders mixed with a few shouts of reprimands from the on-duty teachers was a familiar song. The drum line in his head beat to it: *boomp boomp boomp boomp tat-ta-tat-tat-tat.*

Then, like a record being scratched, every few minutes the teacher in charge jumped on the mic to settle a situation ready to get out of control. The squad cross-talked one another, adding their own bar to the beat. Chris sat across from him, his head bent over his lyric notebook, scribbling. Every now and then, he'd gaze up and look off past Rollie before dipping his head again. Rollie had learned to savor the few snippets of conversation Chris offered.

Mostly Rollie caught pieces of talk with people who stopped by their table, or he listened to the girls go on about everything that came into their heads.

The clock read twelve thirty. In ten minutes Simp would wander in, chill, then roll out before a teacher noticed he was in the wrong lunch. Since Rollie had stopped playing referee between him and Chris, Simp never stayed long. But his appearance was part of the rhythm.

Rollie straddled the bench seating, watching Mo play with Mila's thick wad of braids. Tai slid into place, blocking his view. She sat with her back to him as close as she dared so a teacher wouldn't come by and scold about inappropriate touching. She smelled like baby lotion. He didn't mean to but his nose wrinkled. It didn't stink, but it reminded him of diapers.

"Mo, put it in Bantu knots," Tai said.

"I have too much hair for that. They're gonna look like alien pods," Mila said, eyes bugging.

Tai laughed hard and leaned back into Rollie's chest. She lingered a few seconds, her head resting just below his shoulder. She grabbed his hand from under the table and laid it on her thigh, where it was mostly hidden from the teachers across the room. The warmth of her leg spread through his fingers. He scooted back an inch, letting his hand drop, as the sensation moved through his body. It felt too good. Plus, he knew Mila didn't care about Tai being up on him, but he kind of wished she did.

He'd been thinking about telling her he liked her. Every time he came close, when they were texting, he thought about seeing his words screen shot. Not that Mila would do that but . . . girls shared too much. What if Tai had Mila's phone one day and saw it? It was drama he didn't need.

For now, him and Chris were cool again. He wasn't icing Rollie the way he did Simp—so, it was probably good. Rollie wasn't about to ask. He just rolled with it.

Bottom line, he needed the squad. They'd been even tighter since the Choral Review. He didn't want to mess that up.

Tai's hair swayed gently as his breath blew on her neck. She inched back and he didn't move away this time. Just then, Zahveay slid onto the bench beside Chris, who gave him a look before going back to his book.

Zahveay reached his fist out across the table and

bumped fists with Rollie. "What up, y'all? How the TAG table doing today?"

"Um, hello, everybody here not in TAG," Tai said, raising up.

"You not in it?" Zahveay asked, face pinched in thought.

Tai sucked her teeth. "What gave it away? Me saying everybody here not in TAG."

"Tai dancing with H3 now," Mila said.

"Ay, that's cool. Their videos be popping," Zahveay said, properly in awe. It appeased Tai enough for her to relax back into Rollie.

"Mo, that one knot too big," Tai said as she rolled her eyes at Zah.

"I got this," Mo said, even as she took some of the hair out and redid the knot.

Simp walked up and stood at the far end of the table beside Mo. Zahveay's shoulders sank and he leaned back as if Chris could hide him. His eyes searched everywhere except where Simp was.

"What up, fam?" Simp asked to nobody in particular.

Rollie gave him a head nod. Chris went back to his lyrics.

"Hey, Deontae," Chrissy said. She split open an

orange and held it up, inviting anyone to share. Sheeda was the only taker. The scent filled Rollie's nose, thankfully replacing Tai's baby smell.

"Simp, how do you be getting out of class every day to come down here?" Mo asked. Her hands flew over Mila's head, wrapping the braids into tight balls.

"Nunya," he said.

"Real mature answer," Mo said, rolling her eyes. "I can't with you."

"He got Ms. Jackson. All she care about fourth period is getting her nap in," Tai said. She snored then peeked one eye open before closing it again, sending the squad into a fit of laughter.

"Youn got be putting me out there like that, Tai," Simp said, unsmiling. "People don't be needing to know my secrets."

"Who don't know they can't creep out Ms. Jackson's class, though?" Sheeda said.

"Exactly," Tai said.

Feeling safe in the laughter, Zahveay struck up the nerve to speak. "What up, Simp?

Simp folded his arms. "Ay, yo, what you doing at the Cove table?"

"Simp, don't do that," Mila pleaded. "People should

be able to sit whereever they want. Plus Zah used to be Cove."

Simp's lips turned up. "Used to be."

Chris looked up from his book. "This not even your lunch. Why you care where somebody sit?"

The air was sucked from the entire table. The girls all froze.

Rollie inhaled deep. He nudged Tai. She understood and scooted up so he could swing his leg and sit up right at the table. His knee jiggled as he waited for something to pop off. He'd have to jump in this time, whether he wanted to or not.

He glanced around the room in time to see Marcus and three of his boys roll up beside Simp. They all wore silver-and-black Puma jackets. All of them weren't on the team, but they rocked some kind of silver and black anyway. It was hard to tell if they were a gang or just supporting the team. Anybody with sense knew there wasn't much of a difference.

Zahveay's eyes widened. He sat up straighter, looking from Marcus to Simp.

"We got a problem here?" Marcus asked, eyeing Zahveay then Simp. "I saw you kept looking back at our table. You got something say? I'm right here."

Simp squared his shoulders. "Nah. Just ready put your snitch, Zahvee, up on game and let him know he could run back and tell you—y'all got come better than you did at the J. Martins if you trying win the 'Peake."

Marcus's Adams apple bobbed. It looked like he was ready to unleash. Before he could speak, Zahveay stood up. "Man, look, ain't nobody snitching. Y'all gon' mess around and get in trouble." He nodded his head in the direction of two teachers in conversation then dipped off, feet moving him far away from the thick tension.

"He right, y'all. Ms. Anderson just looked over here," Mo said, pointing.

"Aight den," Marcus said, walking past Simp almost close enough to bump shoulders. His boys followed, doing the same. Simp never flinched. His body was tense, waiting for the slightest touch so he had an excuse to throw hands.

Rollie didn't breathe until the last dude walked by, blessedly far enough away to avoid the brewing fight.

"Why you so mean to Zahveay, Simp? He always been okay with everybody," Sheeda said.

"Then let him be okay with the rest of them marks from the Crossings," Simp said. His head shook in disgust. "Y'all tripping."

"Not me," Tai said, cosigning. "If you hadn't said something, I would have, Simp. Zahveay always been low-key sneaky."

Mila gave Tai a light-lipped frown. Rollie liked how she tried to keep everyone friends. He wanted to do the same thing. But he couldn't keep jumping in and disagreeing with Simp. He flushed with shame when Chris continued to stick up for Zahveay.

"Dude was just sitting here chopping it up. Why y'all care what neighborhood he come from?" Chris asked.

"I mean, I don't," Mo said. She tapped Mila's head to signal she was done. "But the beef between Crossings and the Cove is real. My brother Lenny got suspended off the bus a whole month for fighting DeMarcus, that time. Y'all remember that?"

"But, that was a fight. Do you really not like him just because he moved to a different neighborhood, Deontae?" Chrissy asked.

"I need another reason?" Simp said.

"I mean, kind of." Chrissy tried smiling through her knitted brows. "He seem nice enough."

Simp looked to his right. The Del Rio Crossings' table was deep in the corner. Several of the Pumas were still looking their way. Simp gritted a few seconds longer. Like some kind of bell had gone off sending them to their separate corners, they lost interest and broke eye contact. Simp's head shook. "It ain't my fault Zahvee don't got a set of his own. That's his problem." He shrugged. "You not from here so—"

"Y'all act like we moved here from Mars. We get it." Chris rolled his eyes. "But it's still stupid. I don't like everybody, either, but I got reasons when I don't."

Simp glared at Chris. "Yeah, well, we don't roll like that at B lunch."

Rollie stood up. He had never wanted a teacher to walk by so bad his whole life. He grabbed his backpack from the floor, sat it on the bench, and fiddled with the zipper. He couldn't take sides.

But his muscles, tight and ready to spring, prepared to jump into whatever popped off. He didn't know what was worse—having to jump in if a fight had started with Marcus or now. It was always something.

"For somebody who don't care, you be here every lunch like it's yours," Chris said.

Chrissy squeezed her brother's elbow. "Stop, Chris."

He moved his elbow but stopped short of snatching away. "Naw. Since we not from here, I'm trying hip myself on how they get down in the Cove. That's all."

Simp looked down his nose at Chris. "Youn need worry how Cove get down."

Chris swung his legs around the bench and sprung up. "Yo, is that a threat?"

Rollie was amazed how fast Chrissy got her long legs untangled from under the table. She put her hand on her brother's chest all the while pleading with Simp.

"Can y'all stop? Please. It doesn't have to be this way."

Mila nodded. "Marcus probably laughing knowing he caused beef between us."

"Sit down . . . please," Chrissy said to her brother. He obeyed, keeping his back to the table. The muscles in his neck were tight.

"Look, I ain't the one beefing," Simp said, pouting. "He got a problem with me."

Mo looked from Rollie to Simp to Chris. "What's going on with y'all? What problem?"

"Nothing going on," Rollie said, forcing the words to sound natural. He looked at Simp while he talked. "Everybody not all loved up like y'all."

Tai got loud. "Who's 'y'all'? I wouldn't say we all that."

"Of course you wouldn't," Mo said, with an eye roll so vicious her lashes fluttered a full minute.

"Well, we not, Mo. Keep it one hundred," Tai said, just as huffy.

"But we not sitting here in the caf ready stomp, either," Mo said.

Simp walked around the table and stood in front of Chris. Chrissy looked frightened.

Simp's hand, stiff and in Chris's face, lingered. Finally Chris slid his hand across Simp's and gripped at the fingers. The sun came out on Chrissy's face as she beamed like she'd prevented a world war. But hadn't she?

Rollie's fingers tapped in nervous celebration on top of his backpack.

"Happy now, Mo? Ain't nobody ready stomp," Simp said. "I gotta dip."

"You ain't doing it for me," Mo called after his back. She fixed Rollie and Chris with a stern look. "All I know is, we not jumping into it next time y'all ready brawl. I mean it."

"There won't be a next time," Chrissy said, throwing a look her brother's way.

Rollie didn't know what the twins had agreed on, but Chris's reluctant nod confirmed he'd made some sort of promise. He didn't really understand the bond. He didn't have brothers and sisters—at least none he knew about. But he was thankful for it. Simp and Chris's peace pact was what he needed.

Days later he got up the nerve to admit it to Simp.

He stood on his front stoop and called out, "Oo-oooo." A few houses up, a door opened and Champ stuck his head out. He looked up and down the street, saw Rollie, and hollered back. Rollie threw up the peace sign.

"You good?" Champ called out.

"Yeah. Trying hit up Simp," Rollie called back.

In that moment he loved his hood. Loved knowing that his boys would be there for him from a simple shout. There was movement in Simp's window as someone peeked through the blinds. In seconds Simp was on the step no shoes, no jacket. He immediately looked left then right up the street before exchanging a pound.

"What up?" he asked.

"I needed to holler for a minute," Rollie said. "Hit the Wa with me."

Simp glanced back at the cracked open door. "Ioun

really want leave my brothers right now."

"Oh, it's cool," Rollie said, turning to leave so Simp couldn't see his disappointment.

"Nah. Hold up." Simp hollered back into the house, "Dre, you and Derek get your coats so you can go with me to the Wa. Dom, watch Dee."

"If you can't that's all right," Rollie said, not meaning it.

"You can come in," Simp said.

Rollie unzipped his coat inside the row's stifling heat. Dom was on the couch in shorts and an undershirt. His eyes were glued to the television, which was up too loud.

"You still getting those A's, Dom?" Rollie said.

Dom answered reluctantly, "Yeah."

"That's good, man. Keep doing that," Rollie said, tapping his fist against Dom's.

"Thanks." Dom grinned. "I'm one of the only boys in the Captain's Club."

Rollie wasn't surprised. The small after-school club for kids that got straight A's had been the same way when he was at the elementary school. They had always called them the nerd herd. Nobody was interested in being in it, but everybody secretly hated on them when report cards came out and they got a full-blown pizza party with a DJ. Rollie did fine in school but not straight A fine.

"I told him being the only dude mean he'll get all the honeys," Simp said, smiling proudly.

"True dat," Rollie said.

Dom's nose wrinkled, making them laugh.

"Come on," Simp yelled up the stairs.

Dre sauntered down carrying Little Dee. He dropped him on the sofa and ignored Dee's outstretched arms. Derek bowled past them.

"Can I get a slice of pizza?" he asked, already out the door.

"Ay, stop running," Simp called out. "Dre, keep up with him so he don't run out in the road. We gonna take the long way."

Dre sucked his teeth. "Why we not taking the shortcut? It's cold out here."

"You just be crying about everything," Simp said.

"Ain't nobody crying," Dre said.

The insult had the effect it was supposed to. Dre picked up his pace. He didn't bother to catch up with Derek. Instead, he imitated his big brother's style of barking orders, yelling at his brother to come back.

Rollie waited until they were far enough ahead.

"Ay, yo, look . . . I been tripping a little bit lately," Rollie said. He listened to the thud of their footsteps. The low, steady pounding calmed him. "I was kirkin' on everybody 'cause I couldn't handle mine, for a minute. Know what I mean?" He accepted the nod of Simp's head. "Low-key I was doing too much."

"Wasn't nothing low-key 'bout it, son. That was high-key all day," Simp said. "But I ain't mad at you. You was on your music grind."

"Truth," Rollie said. He slowed his steps when they ventured too close to Dre. Derek's babble filled the air. Rollie couldn't remember how it felt to be seven and be so happy about something as stupid as walking up to the C-store. He sighed and a puff of white air floated in front of his face. "I had real stuff on my mind, though. Son, I tried out for the Rowdy Boys."

He waited for a big reaction but only got a shrug and, "Yeah, Tai told me."

"And that's my bad. You shoulda heard it from me," Rollie said.

The apology lingered between them. As they neared the entrance of the neighborhood, an "Oo-oooo" echoed from a group of their friends standing by the fence.

Rollie and Simp both called back and threw up a fist.

Cars on the main road zoomed by. The swish of their speed overpowered Derek's chatter. Once they rounded the corner, they'd be at the plaza. Once they were out of view of the dudes working the fence, Rollie stopped walking.

"Son, I gotta get out. I can't . . . it's not me," he said. He pulled his hat down so it sat right above his eyes. "I can't even spend the money we be making 'cause you know my moms gonna know something up the second I do. I just feel caught up. I thought if I made the band, that would be my way out. But I ain't on that level yet. I—"

"Ay, it's swazy. For real. I ain't tripping no more." Simp said. He wiped his hand over his face like he was trying to scrub away sadness. "I was at first, though, for real. Man, I thought we was gonna run a whole crew. But, Angel said the game ain't for everybody. And it ain't. No shade."

They gripped, and Rollie felt the weight of the world fall away. He wanted to hold on to the feeling forever. As they pulled away he said. "Can I keep it one hundred?"

"Always," Simp said.

"The game ain't for nobody," Rollie said. He pushed on past Simp's raised eyebrow. "You don't gotta stay down with it, son. If you ball for Sam Well High, you wouldn't be able to play for Tez no more anyway."

Simp's laugh was bitter. "All right, well, we can holler about that if I ever get there."

"Naw, I know," Rollie said. He hadn't meant to bring up Simp being a year behind everybody else. "Just saying, you can get out."

"I don't want get out, though," Simp said. The corners of his mouth were pulled into a tiny smirk. "I'm good at two things—basketball and hustling." He looked past Rollie, shrugging. "And when my mother be needing the money, basketball ain't gonna get that for me. I ain't tripping that you done, though."

Rollie wanted to say more. But what?

He wanted to tell somebody. But who? Simp's mother knew how he got money.

He felt helpless for himself and for Simp, but he let the cold freeze the forced smile on his face.

"What, you giving up on balling in the pros, son?" he asked.

Simp snorted, his grin big. "Never that."

Before his brothers could disappear around the

bend, Simp yelled out to wait. As they caught up, he fantasized about life as a baller, talking about the cars he'd buy, the type of house he'd have. Rollie played along. Loyal as everybody supposedly was to the Cove, getting out was still the goal.

Rollie sent up a silent prayer to Him that somehow both he and Simp would do it.

SIMP

The smell of funky Pampers and burnt bacon smacked Simp in the face as soon as he stepped in Ms. Pat's row. He hopped back out of the way of two little girls running from a little boy waving a plastic bat. They squealed, part terror, part glee, and Ms. Pat yelled from the top of the stairs, "Didn't I tell y'all stop all that screaming?" The bat boy whisper-yelled, "Batter up," and the girls clapped their hands over their mouths to muffle their laughter.

"Ay, Miss Pat," Simp said. He kept his post at the door. Anytime anybody went farther than that, she had a fit talking about nosy people walking through her house. All anybody came by for was to pick up their kids from her wannabe day-care center, but she acted like everybody was the state looking to bust her for not having a license.

"How you doing, Simp?" Ms. Pat came down the stairs, Little Dee in her arms. "His bag right there," she said, pointing to the sofa. At least he assumed it was a sofa under the three diaper bags, a bunch of magazines, and toys.

Little Dee reached for him, calling out with joy, "Thimmmmp."

Simp's heart flipped. He didn't love babysitting at all, but Dee's happiness made Simp feel like he was rescuing him. He had barely scooped Dee's bag onto his shoulder before Ms. Pat dropped his brother into his other arm.

"When your mother gonna pay me?" she asked, cutting her eyes. She pushed a big swath of weave behind her ear, hand on her hip.

"Ioun have nothing to do with that, Ms. Pat," Simp said, boosting Dee up.

Both hands flew to her hips. "Well you gonna have something do with it if I don't get paid and you need stay home from school to watch your brother.

I knew I shouldn't have let your mother slide with paying me late. People make me sick how they take advantage—"

Simp sucked his teeth. "How much she owe you?" He toggled Dee while he went into his pocket. He pulled out a wad of money.

Ms. Pat smiled at the cash. "Umph, look at you." Crying came from a crib in the corner. She looked back at Simp, eyeing the money all the while as she walked away. "She owe me two hundred. You got that much?"

"That's none of your business," he said, without blinking. Sensing he wasn't playing, Ms. Pat frowned but stayed quiet. "How I know she really owe you two hundred?"

Ms. Pat picked up the crying baby and slung it gently onto her shoulder. The gesture didn't match her nasty tone. "It ain't like you can't call or text her and ask. And you know where I live. What I'mma work you out of money for and don't got nowhere to hide from you?" She rolled her eyes at him like it was the dumbest thing she'd ever heard. As she patted the baby's back, her voice lowered. "If I don't get my money today, y'all need find somewhere else for Dee to go."

She glared at him, all the while rubbing the baby's back. Simp stared back, Dee wriggling in his arms. Finally, he peeled off two hundred in crumbled and worn twenties and tens, held the money out, then pulled it back when she reached for it. Her mouth pinched in anger. "For real, Ms. Pat, if I find out you playing me—" He let her make up whatever threat she wanted. It felt weird talking to her that way, but he meant it. He didn't need nobody thinking they could scam him.

She snatched the money. "What I need lie for?" She sniffed as she looked him up and down. There was anger in her face, but fear, too. Still, she didn't back down. "And who you think you are, anyway? I'm grown and you talking to me like that."

"I'm the one who just paid you," he said, stuffing the rest of the money in his pocket as he turned to go. He waited for her or at least her words to follow him out the door. But all he heard was a faint "hmph," and the quiet clunk as she locked her screen door.

"Who she thought she was messing with? Huh, man?" he asked Dee playfully. Dee wrapped his arms around Simp's neck. Simp held him tighter, his stride long. His chest was tight with emotion.

There was a lot he had to teach his brothers about not getting caught up in their hood's nonsense. Whether it was petty beefs or people running game, it was always something you had to look out for.

He dropped Dee's stuff inside the door and yelled for his brothers to come on. Dom immediately groused and begged to stay home alone—at nine he could—but Simp didn't let him. It was too nice out. Still chilly but not cold.

They headed to the basketball courts.

A full game was running on one court. People were standing around, watching and waiting to get on. Another court was full of a bunch of little boys trying to have their own version of the main game. Everybody seemed to be out enjoying the break in the cold. They probably felt the same way about the outdoor courts as Simp—no rules, no refs, just balling as hard as you can. He took his brothers to the empty middle court. Dom reluctantly let himself get pulled into a game with Dre and Derek. They stayed on one end of the court and Simp dribbled the ball with Dee on the other end. The ball was almost bigger than Dee. Every time Simp showed him how to dribble, he picked up the ball and ran. Simp tripped off how he'd run a few steps then stop, usually nowhere near the hoop, then throw the ball.

He took a pic of him and posted it: *Balling like his big bruh already.* Within seconds, Tai had liked it. He grinned stupidly at the little red heart next to his post, laughing at the comments coming in. Some of 'em joking him saying Dee was probably already better than him and a bunch from girls with the same message 😍 🖤 and *aww.*

It was a good day. Probably the first day in a while he didn't feel like there was a gorilla sitting on his back. He knew when it had finally got off him, too—when Rollie told him he wanted out of the game.

He had been scared of hearing those words for months now. And had always thought when he heard them, he'd either end up begging Rollie to stay or be mad at him for punking out. Instead, he'd been grateful that Rollie had told him straight up and to his face. And first, he thought to himself. He told me first.

His burner tickled his right thigh as it buzzed.

It was a 10.10.

Dee shot out from under him and ran toward the

other end of the court.

"Ay, come here," he called out to his brothers, waving them over.

As they approached, Dre taunted Dom. "My point." He pretended to flick the ball at his face.

"I don't care," Dom said, flinching.

"Is it my turn to shoot?" Derek asked.

"It's time to go," Simp said when they encircled him. He picked up Dee, slung him onto his hip.

Dre's mouth immediately drooped. His eyes were hard black beans looking beyond Simp.

"Look, I need go," Simp said in as much apology as he would allow himself. "So y'all need head home."

"Can't Dre take us home after we finish playing?" Derek looked from Simp to Dre.

"I'm ready go, anyway," Dom said. He zipped up his jacket like he'd suddenly gotten a chill.

"Y'all can finish playing in the backyard," Simp said, knowing their shabby hoop wasn't a good substitute for the courts. But it was all he had to offer.

Dre pulled Dee from his arms. "Let's go," he said, walking away without glancing at Simp.

"Can we play when we get home?" Derek asked, skipping to keep up.

Simp watched them go, then turned and went the other way, deeper into the neighborhood.

He tried to forget the steely anger in Dre's eyes. Maybe he could have let his brothers play out their game. Dre would have got 'em all home. But he couldn't risk something happening. What if they got into it with somebody? Somebody was always trying come up by picking on the little kids.

What if Dee got away and ran out in the street? Or Derek—he got faster every day. He had so much energy that letting him outside was like opening a can of shaken soda. His mother would kill him if anybody got hurt, Coach Tez calling him or not.

It was better when they were in the house. That's what it was.

He walked fast, looking straight and about the business. Once he got past the rec center, the building blocked the *ting* of the ball bouncing, the shouts, arguments, and laughter. The Kay didn't just suck the noise out of the Cove, it smothered it. Simp became more alert as he knocked on K-17, its ugly green looking like somebody had dipped a paintbrush in a can of smashed peas. He was surprised when Tez, not his girlfriend Gina, answered the door.

The diamonds in the T on his platinum-capped tooth gleamed at him.

"Ay, little soldier. That was fast."

"I was just at the courts with my brothers," Simp said, tapping his coach's extended fist.

"That's what I'm talking 'bout." Tez nodded, proud. "Look at you, putting in work outside of practice. That 'Peake on lock."

Simp didn't bother to admit he had shot more pics of Dee than balls at the hoop. He stood, his back to the closed door, until Coach Tez invited him to have a seat.

Gina's house was clean. Even though it smelled like fake lemons—like she spent all day cleaning—there was something right under that smell, too. It trailed in and out of his nose, disappearing when he inhaled to get a better feel for it.

He took a seat at a dark wood table, across from his coach. Two long white candles that had never been burned sat in silver holders in the middle of the table. Simp had to keep moving his head to get a full view of Coach Tez's face.

They weren't alone. Coach Tez never was. Upstairs was the *swish-swish-swish* of money in a counting machine. His mind immediately started calculating how much might be sitting just above his head. Coach Tez had at least fifteen people working the street, not counting the 'Rauders. There was probably thousands (hundreds of thousands?) lined up in neat stacks. He wondered if he'd ever be trusted with that job. His hands itched, thinking of being near that much cash.

"Everything good wit' you?" Coach Tez asked.

Unless somebody told you different, Simp thought while saying out loud, "Yeah. Always."

A stack of cash appeared in Coach Tez's hands from beneath the table. The bills, folded neatly over one another, bulged. Without counting, Coach Tez halved the stack and pushed it across the table to Simp. "That's for the last run you did."

Simp pulled the cash to him and stuck it in his pocket.

Coach Tez frowned. "You ain't gonna count it?"

"I trust you, Coach," Simp said, jutting his chin out in what he hoped was confidence.

Coach Tez shook his head. "Nah. When it come to your coins, don't trust no man."

Suddenly Simp didn't have a drop of spit in his mouth. He pulled the cash back out, ashamed, and counted.

"Two hundred?" he asked, regretting the question in his voice.

"Yeah," Coach Tez said, not only disappointed but now bored with the conversation. He barely hid his sigh. "Angel said you be ready run soon. On your own or with a crew. He said you a lot like him. But—" His mouth twisted in thought. He threw his hands up in question then leaned his elbows on the table, peering between the candles. "I still need think on that."

No, I'm ready, Simp screamed in his head. He had wanted to count the money. Knew he should have, but he hadn't wanted Coach Tez to think he didn't trust him. It was a test. It always was. And he'd failed. It took everything to look Coach Tez in the face. He finally blinked, praying his eyes didn't water.

Then as quickly as the storm came, it passed.

"Ay your brother . . . little Pitbull got it all." Coach Tez's head shook, this time in a tiny tic of excitement. His eyes were wide as he reminisced. "Little dude got some real speed on him. And he ain't afraid. He was out there ready throw bows." He chuckled. "Gotta watch that. Can't have him fouling out. I can coach him up, though."

Simp breathed easier. "He been waiting to be down with the 'Rauders for a minute."

"How old is he?" Tez asked.

"He be twelve in July," Simp said carefully.

"That's right, he already supposed to be in middle school." Tez rubbed at his chin. His right eyebrow went up then came back down. "You should have brought him to work out with the team earlier. I would have let him practice with us this year. Get him ready for next season."

Simp had no answer for that. None that he'd ever say to Tez's face anyway.

"Once I put you on to the run, I'mma go ahead and have little Pitbull work the fence with your boy, Rollie. Bring him by to see me, tomorrow."

Simp opened his mouth to say something then sucked his lips in. Even when Tez filled the silence with, "That all right with you?" Simp knew better than to say no.

He swallowed once then again and managed to croak, "Yeah. Yeah, Coach."

Tez stood up. Deep laughter came from upstairs, drawing his attention. He laughed, too, like he knew what was funny. "Counting money put you in a good mood. Know what I'm saying?" He walked to the door. "I want you know that you been killing it on the court. This might be our best team in a long time."

Stupid pride swelled Simp's chest. His thoughts were like cars in a fast lane zigzagging in and out. He was the captain of one of the best teams the 'Rauders ever had. Tez was putting Dre on, like it or not. With Rollie, who was ready to quit.

He couldn't give Tez a heads-up about Rollie. That wouldn't be right.

It was too much.

Next thing he knew, Tez was giving him a pound and a light push to the back and out the door. Simp stood on the front step, looking out at the court. Besides a dude washing his car, no one else was around. Nobody ever came to this court to truly chill. You ain't come to the Kay unless you had to or was ready to get into something you didn't have no business doing. Once you was in the Kay, wasn't nowhere else to go but back out 'cause it was a dead end.

Tez wanted him to bring Dre back here. Back here to nothing.

He gritted his teeth hard enough for pain to shoot up his neck.

He couldn't do this.

He had to do it.

He couldn't.

He had to.

He . . . didn't know anymore.

ROLLIE

Rollie had thought his mother was playing when she said Mr. B was on the phone with news. He'd never had a teacher call his house before. It was weird and got weirder when Mr. B told him that the Rowdy Boys were giving him another tryout.

He was going to get a second chance.

Either there was a whole lot of lame drummers out there or Mr. B was dead-on that something about Rollie's drumming had the band wanting to check him out again.

Now here he was, back in the studio. Luckily, Mr. B had given him a heads-up that this time they wanted him to play with the band. If he hadn't, Rollie would have turned into a straight-up fanboy. Instead, he walked in face neutral, drumsticks in his back pocket. The seven band members looked like any other group of dudes—they were all on their phones till Pee Wee announced him, "All right, fellas, this Ro who I told you about."

Rollie couldn't help himself. A smile dimpled his face. His grandmother's nickname for him should have sounded weird coming out of Pee Wee's mouth. He was like Mr. B, only rounder and a little more hood. Rollie had trusted him on sight. Or maybe it was just knowing he had helped TRB get out the hood and hoping he'd do the same for him. It could still happen, couldn't it? They'd called him back.

He exchanged pounds with the band, reminding himself, with every fist knock and grip, that it was real. He really was standing here talking to B-Roam and Money Mike about what school he went to. They were surprised he wasn't in high school yet. Dat Bass got happy. If Rollie made the band, he wouldn't be the baby anymore.

If.

Them talking like it was possible got the blood

pumping through Rollie's hands.

Pee Wee let them shoot the bo-bo for a few minutes, then clapped his hands. "I like that y'all vibing, but I wanna get this track laid." He flicked a look at Mr. B. "You said he gotta basketball game, right?" He looked down at a big-face watch on his wrist. "How much time we got?"

"I gotta get him out of here at noon," Mr. B said.

Rollie wanted to yell, "I got all day. I don't care about the 'Peake."

But he couldn't do that. When he'd realized that the second audition was the same day as the 'Peake, it made his stomach sick thinking about how to tell Tez. He had immediately told Mr. B and was glad he did because Mr. B talked him through it. The 'Rauders championship game wasn't until afternoon. The audition was early morning. Mr. B would drive him to the auditorium and was even going to stay and watch the game.

"Let's do this then," Pee Wee said.

Him and Mr. B disappeared behind the glass.

"You nervous?" Lips, the horn player, asked.

"All day," Rollie said with a laugh.

"Ride the beat and you be good," Dat Bass said.

Him and Rollie gripped. The other members came up and did the same.

Rollie got settled behind the drums. He clutched the drumstick hard, letting it bite into his hands to stop them from shaking.

B-Roam grabbed the mic stand, rocked it back and forth, and brought the mic up to his lips. "Yeauh. It's your boy Roam back with that fiya."

The second he said "fire," Rollie hit the drum too hard. The note was too harsh. He didn't stop, though. His fingers loosened around the drumstick enough to lighten his touch so that his rhythm rode perfectly under Roam's vocals.

He was doing it.

Twenty minutes later his hands still tingled like they wanted more as him and Mr. B headed to the community college auditorium.

Mr. B had the windows cracked. The cool air wiped at Rollie's brow and his cheeks. He'd worked up a good sweat and probably stank.

"How'd that feel?" Mr. B asked.

"Really good," Rollie said, unable to stop smiling.

He leaned back on the head rest. His body floated.

Even with the 'Peake minutes away, his mind was clear. Once he'd made the decision to quit the team after the tournament, he'd slept better. Did everything better, if the audition was any proof.

"You still might not get invited to join the band. You know that, right?"

"Yeah," Rollie said. He closed his eyes. The jazz Mr. B had playing serenaded him softly.

He could tell Mr. B was looking his way as he asked, "You good with that?"

"I really want to get in," Rollie said. He opened his eyes. "But if I don't, I be good with it . . . probably."

Mr. B's laugh overpowered the sounds of smooth saxophone. "Well, being good 'probably' is better than nothing. You ready for the Pumas?"

"Ready as I'm gonna be." Rollie reached behind his seat and grabbed his big duffel. The campus opened up before them. People streamed by, heading to the auditorium. "Glad the season over after this, though."

He thought about telling Mr. B about quitting basketball. He was curious if Mr. B would think it was the right thing to do. But he was feeling too good. Too much talk about his decision about "basketball" would ruin it. He would rip it on the court today, then call it quits. That's just how it would be.

Mr. B pulled his car into a long line of cars crawling in front of the auditorium. Passengers raced out of the cars and added to themselves to the line snaking out the door. It was the usual madness as people who only cared about the big game merged with folks who had staked out a seat earlier and sat through a few games they hadn't cared about. The car behind them blared its horn when Mr. B took too long to creep his car an inch. Mr. B didn't bat an eye. Didn't even throw his hand (or finger) up at the person. He acted like they had all day.

"You been running a lot this semester. Your grades still holding up?"

"So far. Believe me, G-ma would be making me quit anything but drumming for church if they weren't," Rollie said. Just thinking about how late he stayed up studying just to keep B's and C's made him tired.

"You probably don't want hear it, but you're lucky you have a grandma and mother who stay on you." Mr. B threw one hand up warding off a pretend attack. "And I'm done lecturing." The car had reached the front door. "Have a good game, Roland. I'm risking being permanently banned from the Crossings to root for you."

Rollie laughed. "You sure that's a good idea?"

Mr. B shrugged and winked. "I'll be fine."

"Thanks again for helping me out today. With the ride and stuff," Rollie said.

Mr. B tipped an imaginary hat. "Ball hard."

The college's gymnasium was way larger than where their other games were played. And still it was packed. The lobby was wall-to-wall people as the latecomers waited to file into the already crowded gym. Those near the entrance craned their necks, trying to eagle out a spot. Some people fussed about how slow the line moved. Others talked smack, getting game ready.

He was sure his mother was already in there somewhere. So was the squad. Everybody would either see 'Rauders six-peat or watch them fall back to earth from their streak. Usually seeing the crowd would get him nervous. But it was just a game. Really just a game.

Rollie squeezed through and found the team down a corridor, lounging. He wasn't late, but still expected Simp to be salty. They usually rode together to their games. He was happy when Simp broke his convo with Cappy, put his fist out, and asked, "Everything good?"

Rollie wanted to tell him about the audition, but it was about the 'Peake, right now. He sent up one more silent wish and a prayer, in case He was listening this time, that he'd get the TRB gig, then went to answer Simp.

Tez entered from a side door and hollered at them to come inside the locker room.

As the top seed, they got the home team locker room. The good locker room. Carpeted floors. Tiny monitors all around playing the sports channel. Open, oak "lockers" which were big enough for the shorter players to stand in.

Each player sat in front of what he considered his locker on the shiny oak bench that curved around the entire room. Everybody was subdued. They waited to read Tez's mood to see whether he wanted them excited and serious or excited and loose. Choose the wrong one and—well, no threat of drills since it was the last game—but nobody felt like being yelled at, either.

Tez stood on the giant Warriors' logo, emblazoned red on the black carpet. Coach Monty flanked him. He clapped his hands, yelling "'Rauuuders . . . 'Rauuders . . . " until the team clapped back and answered, "All Day. All Day."

Just like somebody had turned on a faucet, the

locker room grew lively with chatter, chants, and high-fives. Tez let them pump themselves up, then put his hands up for quiet.

"I need my captain come up here." The team applauded as Simp walked up and took his place between Tez and Coach Monty. Once there, he stood at attention, listening intently. Tez put his arm around Simp's shoulder. "I want y'all to know that this little dude, right here, one of the reasons we right back here for the sixth time. No shade to none of y'all, but Simp the hardest-working dude on that floor."

Cappy, J-Roach, and a bunch of the others were eating it up. But Champ's mouth was a thin line. It was a small sign—if you could even call it that—but enough for Rollie. Champ didn't believe anymore, either. Or maybe he was just sick of basketball never being basketball.

If this was about basketball, nobody could take Simp's shine. It wasn't, though. Simp was the next man up. That was the message, in case anybody didn't already know.

Rollie took a deep breath. The rest of Tez's speech droned over his head. A lot of it was him willing them to win. Then there was the low-key threat, "Win big.

Ain't nobody's spot safe on a second-place team." If the others caught that, it didn't dampen their spirits. By the time they hit the floor, all anybody wanted was to do "win big."

The crowd was in a frenzy when the teams jogged out of the locker room. As they stepped to the middle of the court, yells of "'Rauders All Day" and "Puuuma . . . Puma Power" drowned out the referee's directions. Jeers went up as the teams lamely shook hands, a weak sign of sportsmanship that no one really meant.

Marcus and Simp barely touched fists as they eyeballed one another.

Simp bumped chests with Rollie. "We got this?"

"You know it," Rollie said as they gripped.

When the ref's whistle blew and the ball went up in the air, Rollie didn't care about Tez's rah-rah speech or winning big—but the energy flowed from his fingertips to his toes. This was his last game. He was gonna bring it.

The game was ugly from the start.

Reuben was gouged in the eye as he battled for the ball. He swung at the dude that poked him. The referee blew his whistle loud and long. He put his hands up, blew again until the crowd hushed. He bellowed so the crowd heard every word.

"We're not doing this today, fellas. I'll clear this entire gym if I have to—fans, coaches, everybody. I mean it."

There were a few boos as the ref called a technical foul on Reuben. Rollie tapped Reuben on the butt. "Don't let 'em get to you, man."

Tez paced the sideline, staying smartly quiet.

As Slink took the shots for the Pumas, Simp gathered the team into a loose huddle.

"Y'all got keep your head, for real. Don't be giving 'em points," he said.

"Dude poked me in my damned eye," Reuben said, scowling.

"Y'all can handle that in the street then. For now, let's just take it to 'em," Simp said.

A look of disgust flashed across Reuben's face, but he dapped up Simp's outstretched hand.

"Let's go," Rollie said.

The scuffle ramped up the crowd, but calmed the teams—the tension between them masked in focus.

By the second half, Rollie's heart was beating so fast his throat ached. Neither team was giving up. He leaned deep inside the huddle to hear better. The team's collective funk was a thick, humid musk in his nose separate from his own. But he didn't mind. Together they'd almost climbed out of a twelve-point deficit. Now with only seconds left on the clock, they had a chance to pull ahead and win it. With their sweaty bodies pressed against one another, they were one beating heart. In the middle, Tez drew a play on his clipboard. Even with him yelling, it felt like he was speaking regularly. Rollie pressed in until his words were clear.

"I think they gon' pull an okey-doke on us and switch to zone," Tez said. "We gonna let 'em play they selves. Rollie, do what you gotta do to get open. Simp, take it in like you going for the shot. Play it up. I want all their eyes on you." His voice hardened. "Watch the clock, though. Once Rollie open, pass and let him sink it." He gazed up at Rollie and nodded in affirmation for an answer never spoken. "Just sink it, pretty."

Rollie's heart banged in his chest. Tez was putting this all on him. If he got two points, they'd tie it up. The thought of battling in overtime made his stomach churn. If he sunk the three-point shot, the 'Rauders won. But if he missed? The Pumas would eat up the time left and walk away champions. He felt Simp pound his shoulder. Heard his teammates growl, "'Rauders All

Day." But his mind was already going over the shot in his head. He could feel the ball in his hands. Saw the net shiver as the ball slid through.

It was like drumming. Feel it then do it.

The whistle blew.

Tez was right. After playing the entire game man-to-man, every Puma was protecting their one little piece of the court. Rollie grit his teeth to keep a smile from spreading. He threw the ball in and took his place like he was about to let Simp be the star of the show. Expecting this, Pumas sent two dudes at him. They were smooth with it, boxing Simp out like he was the sun trying to shine through thick gray clouds.

Open, Champ clapped for the ball. It drew the dude covering him to step in tighter. No one was worried about Rollie. The man covering him either figured they weren't going to get any action or was confident that whoever their rebound man was would get him the ball in time. He was probably already celebrating in his mind when Rollie whipped past him and caught the ball. By the time Rollie was midair, his man was two seconds too late.

The ball floated from Rollie's hands. With his hands arced in perfect form, he watched as the rock flew then swished effortlessly into the net. His teammates swooped in. Simp scooped him up and swung him around. The crowd went nuts.

The gym filled with "'Rauders All Day. 'Rauders All Day."

They'd won. They were six times 'Peake champs.

Rauders 75, Pumas 74

When it was over, all Rollie wanted to know was, what would Tez have done with the new jackets if they hadn't won? They had been waiting for them in their lockers after the game, shiny, gold, and bright. Everybody was so excited, nobody had asked—what if we had lost?

Rollie felt stupid for being the only one who wondered.

A week later he was still thinking about it as he headed to the shed, where Tez had agreed to meet him.

The jackets were gold, real gold not yellow gold, with black embroidered lettering. One sleeve had his number. The other had all six years that they'd won the 'Peake running down to the elbow. His name shimmered on the front and under it in quotes was Tez's new nickname for him, "Silent But Deadly." It wasn't so much a nickname as a description, but Tez had been so proud, announcing it, that all Rollie could do was smile and pretend he liked it.

He had the jacket draped over his arm. He couldn't accept it. It was bad enough he had felt like a fraud celebrating with everybody. Yeah, he'd helped the team win. Had helped them big by putting up twenty-five points. But when he was jumping around, embracing his teammates, shooting water at them, it was from relief.

He was done.

His feet picked up the pace, knowing he was finally ready to get out.

The Cove was bustling. Friday nights always were, but with the win it was a new layer of busy. The hood had put the 'Rauders up on their shoulder, rooting them to the win, and tomorrow Tez would repay everyone with a huge winter block party. Tables and makeshift grills of concrete blocks were already set out. The only thing better than a summer cookout was a winter one—any excuse to come out and show out. Every group he passed shouted out congratulations or "good game."

Rollie let himself enjoy it. Everybody assumed he'd make the Sam Well High School team and was already fantasizing about it. Another Cove basketball star on the come up. He let them. Sooner or later the grapevine would find out he wasn't trying out. He needed a break from basketball.

First thing he saw when he got to the rec was Simp and Cappy. They sat on the low wall, watching the traffic slow roll by. Both had on their jackets, which were bright in the dark night. For a second, Rollie wished he'd worn his instead of carrying it. His worry about anyone caring were quickly dashed when Cappy, with his face in his phone, only gave Rollie a nod before walking a few feet down to a stopped car. He leaned, his head just outside its window, said something, laughed, and gave the person in the passenger seat a quick grip.

"Roll-lay," Simp called out. He was off the wall in an instant, his arms open for a pound.

Rollie gestured to Cappy. "Y'all working?"

"He is. I'm just chilling," Simp said. His warmness zapped away like the sun disappearing behind a cloud.

First rule of the game: Don't talk about the game. Especially to people who not in the game . . . anymore.

It hurt Rollie's feelings. It would be a stone-cold lie to say it didn't. Already he was just another mark. That's how it was going to be now?

He switched the subject, hoped his face didn't look as broken as it felt.

"You ain't never hit the chat. You know the squad cooling over Chris and Chrissy's tonight, right? You down?"

"Yeah, I saw. Naw. I'm good," Simp said. His eyes looked over Rollie's head, checking out the action on the street and sidewalk. Same as always. Rollie wasn't sure Simp even knew he was doing it.

Cappy passed by and exchanged a fist bump with Rollie as he took his place back on the wall.

"Thought you and Chris was all right, now? You should slide through," Rollie said.

Simp's face went through a few emotions at once, like the computer in his brain was having a hard time processing whether to be amused, irritated, or torn.

"Yeah we good," Simp said, finally. "Iouno, I might roll through. I hit you up if I do." He put his hand out and Rollie gave it a grip. He felt even more cracked when Simp hit him with a dismissive, "All right then," and headed back to the wall, where a small group of girls was talking to Cappy.

Rollie recognized two of them. They were sixth graders.

One of them was challenging Cappy, asking all loud why she couldn't try on his jacket and he was going off more than he needed to, loving the attention. Rollie turned his back and started the walk to the team's equipment shed. The girls' high giggles made him want to turn around to see if they were laughing at him. He resisted, kept one foot in front of the other as the sidewalk led from the well-lit front to the shadowy side of the rec building.

If this was how it was going to be between him and Simp, him and any of his teammates once he officially left the game, it sucked. He wasn't ready to feel like a stranger in the only neighborhood he knew. He didn't go around beefing with people, but knowing a whole squad of dudes had his back if he did was like an invisible cloak—after a while what you did, how you acted was because you knew you had it on. He wasn't just taking off the cloak, he was wiping away any protection it had ever given him.

Right before he hit the shed, he put the 'Rauders jacket on over his sweatshirt and zipped it all the way up like it would keep out the thoughts clouding his mind. Suddenly it felt like a bad idea to bust up into the shed without it on.

When he heard footsteps, he figured it was Simp. He smiled, thinking, He came to stand by me while I tell Tez. Ready to admit how scared he was, he swiveled around and nearly walked into Zahveay.

It was enough light for him to see his face clearly. Still he squinted, confused.

"Man, what the—" He checked behind Zahveay, expecting someone to be with him. When he saw they were alone, he reprimanded him, "Don't be sliding up behind me like that. What's wrong with you?"

Zahveay showed him his hands. "My bad. I called out to you, back there, but I guess you didn't hear me."

Rollie looked "back there." They were only ten feet from the shed, but a good thirty yards from the commotion on the street. If Zah had called him, he would have heard him. It was dead quiet back this deep.

His muscles went tight. "What you want, son?"

"I never got to say congratulations. Y'all did that last Saturday." Zahveay shoved his fist toward Rollie. When Rollie went to tap it, Zah grabbed his fist and pulled him in close.

Rollie pushed him with his free arm, but Zah's grip was tight. They were so close, he smelled onions on Zah's breath.

"What you doing, yo?"

"This ain't personal, all right?" Zah said. For a second his eyes seemed to apologize, but then went flat again. "I gotta do what I gotta do."

Rollie's jaw tightened. Whatever was going on right now would be over in a minute. He'd let Zah say what he needed to. When it was over though . . . he already envisioned his free hand swinging at dude's face. He was going to rock him.

He licked his lips, working to look like this didn't faze him, even as his heart pounded.

"Everybody know Tez keep money in the shed," Zah said.

Rollie made his voice, flat, uninterested. "Everybody who?"

"Don't play me, son." Zah gripped tighter and Rollie fought not to wince. For being a small dude, his squeeze was strong. "I know you one of his boys. Get me in there and nobody gotta get hurt."

"Ay, look, I can't do nothing for you. You rolled through here over some rumor about money in the shed?" Rollie asked, calmer than he felt.

Money in the shed. Bulletproof walls. A safe full of drugs. Those were the types of rumors that people spread about the place the 'Rauders kept their equipment. It wasn't funny, because Zah looked dead serious, but Rollie forced a laugh up his throat. "You wylin'."

"Rollie, this ain't no joke, son. I ain't no joke."

"Whatever, man. If you all that, go right ahead and walk in the shed. It's open. See if Tez don't light you up."

As Zah stared at the shed door, debating, his grip loosened enough for Rollie to snatch away. The move startled Zah. He looked from Rollie to the door, his hand struggling to get something out of his jacket pocket.

With a gun at his face, Rollie put his hands up. "What you—" was as far as he got when there was a pop. No, it was a crack—a mini crack of lightning exploding and striking his leg.

He stumbled back, crashed into the shed's door, and fell. He tried to use his good leg to boost himself up, but the pain in his other leg blazed. It hurt too much to move. He watched as Zah faded into a silhouette then nothingness into the black of the trees.

The darkness shimmered. He blinked, trying to bring it back into focus. His leg was hot and cold. The heat suddenly raged as Tez burst out the shed door, bumping against Rollie.

Tez was waving something as he barked, "What happened?"

"Lightning," Rollie said. But he wasn't sure he was saying it aloud because Tez kept asking the question.

Rollie closed his eyes. When he looked up, again, the faces had multiplied. This had to be what fish in a bowl felt like, faces wavering above them. Everybody had the same wide-eyed look, like it was work to peer through the water at him.

He closed his eyes trying to stop the blurring. How come nobody was helping him up?

If he had help, he could at least stand on his good leg.

In his mind, he reached his arm out to signal them to help. Somehow, next thing he knew when he opened his eyes again, Simp was there gesturing, pointing toward the woods. Rollie wanted to turn and see what was in the woods. But knew better. Movement was bad. Plus, it was wet under him. He felt frozen to the ground.

He would never live it down if he had peed himself.

Simp squatted beside him.

Finally, somebody was helping him up.

Rollie went to lift his arm, but it was too heavy. He

was suddenly fighting to keep his eyes open.

Simp scooted behind Rollie, gently pulling trying to prop him up. The heat in Rollie's leg exploded and he screamed loud, long, and deep. He screamed like someone was stabbing his leg with hot metal pokers. He screamed like someone had broken glass inside his skin.

He screamed like he'd been shot. Because he'd been shot.

Zahveay had shot him and the wetness was blood. His blood. He couldn't see it. God, he was so glad he couldn't see it. Because just knowing it was there spilling all over the sidewalk made him want to throw up. His stomach seized then released, and vomit spewed from his mouth down the new shininess of his jacket.

Behind him, Simp was wimpering, "Son, it's gonna be all right. You gonna be all right."

The shimmering faces were shouting at each other about nine-one-one. And all Rollie wanted was for his g-ma to rub his temples. When he was little he'd lay his head on her lap at church and she'd rub his temples until he drifted off to sleep. One time he went to lie down and she scolded him. "Five years old is old enough to start listening to the sermon." That's when

Rollie had stopped liking church as much—at least until he started playing drums instead. He wished G-ma and her soft warm hands were there. It was freezing on the sidewalk.

"We gon' get them fools," Cappy said. He swiped at the tears leaking from his eyes. He peered around like he had lost something then tapped on his phone. Every time it lit up it seemed another person arrived. So many people. None of them his g-ma. He wanted to tell Simp to call her, ask if she'd rub his temples.

He could barely hold his eyes open anymore. He wanted to sleep and could if it wasn't so cold on the ground. If somebody could just move him or give him a blanket, he'd be all right.

"I'mma be all right," he muttered.

Simp jiggled him. "Rollie? What you say, man? Stay with me, son."

The pain stabbed at him. He screamed, "Man, stop moving. Please, stop moving," but only in his head. He knew now he wasn't saying anything they understood. Still he slurred again, "Ah be all righh if oo stah mooing."

"I can't understand you, son," Simp said. He sounded like he was talking through a mouth full of water. "Who did this? Who shot you, Rollie?"

Rollie worked at forming Zah's name. He pushed his tongue down, willing the word to come out right. It came out a hushed sigh, "Sah."

Simp asked over and over, "Who shot you?"

Rollie gave up. He just needed to sleep for a few minutes. They could talk about it later. He hoped they'd wait for him before they served Zahveay the whipping he deserved. He was too tired to do it right now. But once he caught this nap . . .

EPILOGUE—
SIMP'S APRIL

For the Cove Marauders, if winter was about showing out, then spring was about showing off. Tryouts were a community affair. A time for everyone to see what "their" team might look like. Literally, since tryouts were held in the outside center court.

It was a public practice with plenty of drills and everything from full-court scrimmages to half-court one-on-one. Pressed parents, boy-crazy girls, and wannabe sports analysts showed up to see which boys ages eleven to thirteen had what it took to be a rough ride 'Rauder.

Twenty-five dudes were trying out for the team's six open slots. They would spend the whole day ripping and racing up the court, taking orders from assistant coaches and veteran players. Some would be sidelined by cramps. Some would give up the ghost (the breakfast and their lunch, too) on the sideline then get back out there. Others would simply drop out. And being the last man standing only counted if you were good enough with the rock. If you earned a spot, you were played hard during the summer league games. By the time the actual season started in November, even the newest player would feel like a veteran. But first, tryouts.

The returning players were on the court working as assistants to the assistant coaches and scrimmaging on demand. One minute they were correcting a boy on his technique, the next they were guarding that same boy at the blow of a whistle. The whistle commanded all, except the captain. He was exempt from the circus-like atmosphere. The reward for being "king."

Simp sat on the silver bleacher on the sidelines, alone. He was geared up, just in case Tez asked him to demonstrate something. But Tez wouldn't. Sitting on the sidelines let everybody know he was the man. Still, secretly he was down to jump in on a scrimmage.

Behind him, the crowd was festive. About fifty onlookers were dotted along the bleachers, picnic tables, and grass surrounding the court. It was only eleven a.m. but a few dudes were passing around a bottle wrapped in a brown bag. Simp doubted it was orange juice. Every few minutes somebody would yell out encouragement to their son, nephew, or the kid they'd put a side bet on.

Anybody watching, with sense, would be betting on Dre.

So far that day, he'd been vicious on defense and was beast anytime he had the ball. Simp had heard somebody yell, "Ay, is that little shorty from fifth court? Simp's brother," and after Dre had stolen the ball and taken it full court for a layup, "Little dude right there got the goods."

Dre wasn't trying out to make the team; he was trying out so Tez could show the hood that he still drew the best talent and most dedicated players. Who else would put themselves through this?

It was a daylong commercial for the Marauders. When it ended, only the best would stand and every one of them would wear that label like a badge of honor. After spewing their guts on the court, burning under the spring sun, and running for four hours, they wouldn't just be ready to play, they'd be ready to go to war for Coach Tez.

Knowing that, Simp had made a decision. Angel had given him the idea. If Raheem had told Tez no, then so could he. At least for his little brother he could.

It had been on his mind ever since Angel told him the story. He just hadn't known what to do with it . . . until Rollie got shot.

It still blew him. Shot. Over an imaginary safe.

Simp hadn't known anybody still really believed that stuff about the shed having a safe or money in it. It was street talk, always had been. But those fools from the Crossings had believed it and got Zahvee's dumb butt to stick it up, promising him he could be down with them if he did. Rollie had just been in the wrong place. It could have been anybody. It could have even been Dre.

Simp grit his teeth back and forth. Revenge still wired his body every time he thought about it. It wasn't going to be Dre.

Telling Tez hadn't been easy. Maybe in the end,

he'd only agreed because he was still so high on the 'Peake win. Simp didn't know. Didn't care.

He watched his brother on the court. Dre must have forgotten he was in a tryout. He was street balling, dribbling the ball in between his legs and taking chances that most coaches would have whistled him down for. Not Tez. Tez hadn't taken his eyes off Dre. He kept dapping up Coach Monty anytime Dre did something. Anybody watching knew Dre was a favorite.

Simp was cool with him being the favorite as long as it was just on the court.

He still couldn't believe he'd stood up to Tez. He'd texted him 10.10, not sure how else to let him know he had business to talk about. When he'd gotten back to the shed, he'd had to step over Rollie's dried blood still in front of the door. It made his stomach flip. But it gave him the courage he needed. He couldn't have his little brother's blood on somebody's sidewalk over drug money.

Tez had this smirk on his face. Had his elbows on his desk, his head resting on his hands, like he was in for a good show. He'd practically been chuckling when he asked, "What's up, little soldier?"

Simp had hit him with it straight.

"I don't want Dre hustling." Tez's head had reared back. Simp filled in the space left by his surprised silence. "He wanna be down with the team. You already said he good enough for that. But I don't want him hustling. I just don't, Coach."

His chest had been heaving from the effort. He ignored his own fear. This was for Dre. Dre, who didn't know he was doing this. Dre, who was probably going to be mad he was doing this.

Tez had gestured to the one chair open in front of the desk. "You amped right now, huh? Didn't come in say hey, how you doing or nothing. Just putting me on notice about who can or can't work for me." His eyebrow slid up. This was when Simp was supposed to back down. He knew it. But he hadn't.

He sat down. Took a few breaths. "It's plenty of other cats who can run for you. I just don't want my brother being one of 'em."

"You the last word on that?" Tez asked.

And for a second, Simp wondered if his mother had already talked to Tez. She didn't know he was doing this, either. And it shook him that she would undo what he was trying to fix.

He couldn't make it right for Rollie. He could

for Dre, so he'd lied and confirmed he was the last word, praying his mother wouldn't make him look cracked by overruling him.

Tez had sat back, hand still folded under his chin. For the first time, Simp felt anger at his coach. He wasn't asking Tez to leave Dre alone; he was telling him. His anger must have shown on his face because Tez had put his hand up before Simp could open his mouth.

"Look, if you don't have the stomach for this no more. That's cool. The game—"

"Ain't for everybody," Simp finished for him, relishing the look of openmouthed shock on Tez's face. "Yeah. I know. And it's not for Dre. That's all I'm saying."

Tez's head fell back as he laughed. "You serious, huh?"

"Dead," Simp had said.

A few awkward silent moments followed before Tez's head bobbed up and down. "It's good, little soldier. It's good. You still my general, right?"

It was the one moment Simp would play over again in his mind. Had Tez really been offering him a way out or had it been another test?

He wasn't the thinker. Thinking wasn't what had him in the shed speaking up for Dre. He loved his brother. His job was to protect him. Protecting him was as built into him as dribbling down the court for a layup. Thinking was different. It wasn't always easy for him. He'd hesitated, but only a second before he'd answered, "Yeah, Coach. I'm still your man."

The order was back after that. Tez was the teacher. Simp was the student.

"It's a lot of people around here who don't want their kids playing for me. They're the ones who the rec league take. Sloppy seconds." Tez shrugged, like he really didn't understand why anyone would pass up his team. "But there's this kid from the Kay. His mother wouldn't let him try out last year or the year before. But guess who already signed up for spring tryouts?" His deep laugh filled the small shed. "That's right. Little shorty be there this year. Heard he bad, too. But that ain't the point. I'm cool with Dre only putting in work on the court. 'Cause the point is, for every kid that don't want get in the game with me there's five, ten others that will. It's about that cream, little soldier. All about that cream."

C.R.E.A.M.

Simp knew it meant *cash rules everything around me*. Where was the lie?

Cream was why he'd just signed up for a new tour of duty under Tez. He wasn't going anywhere, no time soon. But maybe one day. For now? For now, keeping his brother out the game was the only win he needed.

EPILOGUE—
ROLLIE'S APRIL

Forty.

That's how many times Rollie had heard the phrase, "It could have been worse." And every time he felt like screaming, "Then you try getting shot."

It wasn't that he didn't understand that it could have been worse. Nobody was going to get an argument from him that a broken leg from a bullet was better than death by a bullet. Still, people could miss him with that "could have been worse" mess. People who said that had never had their leg catch fire. Had never sat in their own blood freezing to the ground. Had never experienced seeing their leg flop where it should have been upright. And now, he also had a gift he'd have forever—a metal rod in his leg. Already he'd had to take a note to school to explain why he would always set off the metal detectors. So yeah, it could have been worse, but it wasn't no party, either.

A thought he kept to himself around his g-ma. Every blessing at dinner included an extra two minutes dedicated to how thankful she was that He had spared Rollie. And Rollie wanted to believe He had something to do with it. But, secretly, he felt like Zahveay had gotten scared or had bad aim. He didn't know which. Didn't want to know. Thinking about quiet, tap-dancing Zahveay shooting him made him feel . . . stupid. He should have listened to Simp. Should have paid attention to Zah talking him up, the way he had.

Now look at them—the jailbird and the gimp.

Zah was in juvenile lockup awaiting trial on attempted murder. Seeing that in the papers and knowing it was his life Zah had attempted to take shook Rollie. He had avoided newspapers and the TV for two weeks because he couldn't hear about it anymore. That had been hard to do since he'd been laid up in bed with nothing else but TV and his phone.

Now he was on crutches for the next six weeks. He even needed help in the shower. No amount of explaining made his mother understand that he did not want it to be her. He'd stay dirty for six weeks if that was his only option. It was a little better having his cousin Michael help him. But only a little.

The mess was embarrassing.

In three more weeks he'd get the cast off. The doctor had warned him—no basketball next season (he hadn't planned on it) and that he'd have to ease back into drumming. At that, Rollie had protested. He hadn't been shot in the leg he used for the bass drum (okay, that was a good thing, so he gave Him that one). He didn't understand why he couldn't get right back to it. But there had been a whole bunch of talk about possible damage to his nerves and giving the leg time to truly heal. He didn't have time. The Rowdy Boys were waiting on him. If he took too long to heal, they'd move on.

They'd picked him. Said he was the one. This chance would never come back a third time.

He explained that to his mother. To G-ma. Even to the doctor.

Of course, G-ma's answer was, "If that's His will,

Ro, then they'll wait."

Ever since then he'd had a short talk with God every night. "If You really up there, please let this be Your will. I need them to wait. I need this dub."

He wondered if God knew that he was on the fence about believing in Him? Hoped he didn't because then He might not be as willing to grant Rollie this solid. All he could do was wait and see.

Meanwhile, him and his mother were living with G-ma's sister in the Woods until his mother could get everything straight for them to move from the Cove. He shared his older cousin Michael's basement bedroom. If you could call him sleeping on the couch sharing.

On one whole side of the room, sketches of clothes Michael had designed were posted all around. He even had one of those headless mannequins draped in fabric. That was definitely creepy. But Michael was mad talented. Some nights, the two of them stayed up late talking about how famous they'd be one day—Michael in fashion, Rollie in music.

Rollie didn't even care if he got famous as long as he could keep drumming. He missed it.

He thought he'd miss the hood, too. He'd been wrong. The Woods was a predominately Black neighborhood.

It was like the Cove's fraternal twin—different in a lot of ways, but also a little familiar. And he still got to see the squad, for now, because his mother dropped him to school every day.

He'd already made her promise that no matter where they moved, he could stay in TAG. He felt a little bad for making her promise. She was already doing so much to get them out of the Cove. No way she was going back to live where her baby had almost been killed—words that made Rollie's skin break out in goose bumps. He knew she meant it, but he still hadn't rested until she'd promised.

Michael's voice came to him from the other side of the room. "Did you hear anything I said, man?"

Rollie shook the cobwebs off. "My bad. Naw."

"I was saying that Cinny's little sister should be a model. She's the perfect height. Ask her if she'd come over here and let me try some stuff on her."

"That's word," Rollie said, pretending that mention of Mila didn't make his heart dance a little bit. He pulled out his phone and texted her right away, glad to have a reason to.

He'd talked to Mila more than anybody since moving. Her sister and auntie were just down the road from his cousin Michael's house. She'd spent a whole summer on this side of town. They talked about that a lot. That and TAG and summer, never about the night he'd been shot. Right now, she was the only person who seemed to understand he didn't want to spend every second of the day remembering it. He didn't want to spend any part of the day remembering it, but some things slammed it into his head anyway—loud noises, footsteps behind him, and the cold. Even when he was wrapped in a blanket, he could feel the freezing concrete of the sidewalk seeping into his bones.

He shuddered, stamping out the feeling before it took hold.

Everybody didn't get that he wanted to move on. Definitely Tai didn't get it. Once he'd finally gotten off painkillers and wasn't off in la-la land half the time, Tai had burned his phone up. But all she wanted to talk about was how it had felt to get shot (it hurt) and how the streets were talking about how it was Zah that had done it (sometimes rumors be right). It was like she was trying to be the first to get the scoop. Then she'd gotten all in her feelings when he bassed on her with, "Look, if that's all we gonna talk about, I need go."

She'd cut back calling after that and now barely

texted him. When he was out of sight, he was out of her mind. How messed up was that?

When he'd first gotten back to school it went from her appointing herself his personal nurse—walking with him to class—to her being annoyed that he took too long on the crutches and made her late for her class. It had been at least a week since they'd talked outside the squad's chats or lunch. And he was good with that.

He'd had a lot of time to think while he was laid out on the basement sofa. One thing he was starting to understand—little things connected people, but they didn't always make you real friends.

He hoped that wouldn't happen with Simp. So far, Simp was still his boy.

The way Simp had held him, that night, crying, still made Rollie want to cry sometimes. If he had died . . . His throat closed up.

From across the room, Michael wasn't paying him any mind as he sketched something. Rollie turned the channel, pretending to be looking for something to watch until the lump in his throat went away. The thing was, Simp could have been the last person he heard before he died. He thought about this more than he wanted to. Simp had his back that night. Rollie would always love him for that.

He hadn't been allowed a lot of visitors, but Simp had visited him in the hospital almost every day. Rollie had been pretty drugged up on the meds, so his memory on the visits were fuzzy. Some might have been dreams. One day stuck with him. He figured it must have really happened.

Simp had come to tell him that leecee had gotten Zah, who had been hiding out at a relative's. The news didn't make Rollie happy. It meant more talk at school. More news clips. But he was glad it was over. He figured Simp was telling him because he was glad, too. Instead, Simp had been annoyed. "Did you ever tell 'em who shot you?"

When Rollie admitted he had, Simp had glowered. "Man, me and Cappy was gonna take care of that for you. You should have just said it was too dark to see."

Rollie remembered feeling angry as he explained, "My mother was here when the cops talked to me. She wouldn't have been down with that no snitching mess, man."

The hard scowl on Simp's face crumbled. He turned his head and swiped at his eyes. When he turned back around his eyes were dry. He had a smile on his face, but it looked like it hurt him to do it. "That punk got lucky, then. Know what I mean?"

He reached for Rollie's hand and gripped it lightly, like he was afraid Rollie would break if he held on too tight. Yet, he held on a few more seconds before knocking elbows with Rollie. "Be all right, hear?"

"Naw, you be all right," Rollie had said, wishing like a kid on a star that something, somebody would protect his friend out there on the streets.

"Oh, I'mma be all right." Simp's platinum cap shone at him. "Check on me sometimes, though."

Rollie had dazed out after that. Half remembering, half dreaming about how his mother absolutely wasn't about to let him follow some code of the street. When the cops talked to him, he had been too busy praying they didn't have any kind of information about his work with Tez to worry about not snitching. They hadn't. They had seemed genuinely interested in solving the case and had been surprised when Rollie said he'd known who did it. Or maybe they were surprised that Rollie had told. Everybody else sure was.

Some of his old "friends" were treating him differently. Probably some of it was because he'd told. Some of it though, was because he wasn't in the Cove with them anymore and wouldn't be back. Five weeks and he was already an outsider, it seemed. If he'd been back in the hood, he would have been a hero probably. Leaving meant he wasn't Cove anymore. Moving was for suckers.

He didn't spend time worrying about it. Simp and the squad (most of the squad) was still checking for him. Right now, that's all that mattered. Everybody else?

Anybody who wasn't checking for him because he'd had the nerve not to die in the street and be the story they talked about, the "in memory" patch they wore on their jerseys, the "RIP Rollie" messages on social media—as far as Rollie was concerned, those people were cobwebs. He'd walked into them and for a while they stuck to him, stuck to him good. But once he finally brushed them away, they lost their hold.

The Cove had lost its hold on him. He almost didn't get out alive. But as Mr. B had told him, almost doesn't count.

He wasn't looking back anymore.

Keep reading
for an exclusive look.

RASHEEDA

The Summer of Lonely.

The Lonely Summer.

She wasn't sure which one to call it.

The second that her best friend, Mo, had come to her, excited about getting into something they called an "intensive" (why not just call it "dance camp," for real?), Sheeda's summer was turned on its head. But then Mila got in, too. And Chrissy was going away to spend time with family in Virginia. The entire squad was ghost for the summer. That just left her.

Well, and Tai. Tai wasn't going anywhere. Low-key, a summer with Tai, who had exactly one speed—bossy—

wasn't any better than a summer totally alone.

Rasheeda Tate hadn't had a Lonely Summer (That sounded better. Summer of Lonely was too fancy.) since her very first in the Cove. It was home now. She almost, *almost* couldn't remember a time when it wasn't.

When she first left North Carolina to move in with her aunt, she mumbled to hide her slow drawl to fit in with the Cove kids whose words streamed strung together. Mo was the one who hadn't teased her. Who had taught her the dead-eye stare when grown men hollered, "Hey, little momma, what's your name?" Mo was the one who stood up to older girls who ordered them to do stupid stuff, like fetch snacks from the Wa.

The last six summers were hanging together out at the basketball court, even when it was scorching hot.

Going to the carnival together and eating funnel cake until the powdered sugar gave them a headache.

Hanging out at the rec's open gym nights with their squad.

Now what was she going to do?

Stupid question. Because she was going to end up in church every day. Just like she was at this moment, sitting lonely in the second pew waiting until Sister Butler made everyone stop all the foolishness and get up in the choir loft. Sheeda knew she looked antisocial. Good, 'cause she felt that way.

For real, it always took her a few minutes to be all right with being stuck at church. Today she was feeling more standoffish than usual. Yola and Kita, her two closest church friends, were used to it and let her be until she felt like dragging herself up the three tiny stairs that led to where the choir sat staring out into the big sanctuary. Sitting alone on the long pew that could hold fifteen people, while everybody else bulled around, Sheeda might as well have been invisible.

Again.

Just like when she hadn't made it into TAG.

Jealousy burned her chest. She didn't want it to. But it did.

She danced, too. Not that anybody would know it, since she was the only one in their clique whose dancing wasn't good enough outside of church. That's how it felt. She'd been praise dancing for years and was good. Still, it hadn't gotten her into the school's talented and gifted dance program. Now Mila and Mo were going away for three weeks to dance. And Sheeda was bursting with why's. Why hadn't she been good enough to get into TAG dance? Why hadn't their dance teacher from the rec center at least recommended her for the summer intensive thingie? And why in the world had she been stupid enough to admit how she'd felt to her aunt?

Auntie D wasn't having any of her whining. She'd put her hands on her slim, barely there hips and said, "Rasheeda Tate, listen to yourself. The Bible says, 'But each person is tempted when they are dragged away by their own evil desire and enticed.'"

Sheeda had wiped her face of any expression. Her aunt paused, just enough to let the Bible verse sink in. "That's from James, first chapter, fourteenth verse. If He wanted you in that school program for dance, you would have gotten in. Nothing good is going to come from you wanting something that wasn't meant to be."

Usually after a lecture, Sheeda thought about doing better. Not that time. Evil desire. Really? She'd been dancing at church forever and everybody swore she was good, but now, suddenly, wanting to dance was evil?

She'd almost said as much to her aunt. Instead, she'd quietly muttered, "Yes, ma'am." There was no point. When Deandra Tate's mind was made up, it was a wrap.

With no alternatives for summer, Auntie D would 100 percent fill any free second Sheeda had with church. And Sheeda hated that she didn't have any choice in it.

Hated it like a chair scraping across the floor. Hated it like when the teacher volunteers you to read something out loud because she can sense you don't want to. Hated everything about the never-ending schedule of choir and praise dance rehearsals, youth activities, Bible study—repeat, repeat, repeat.

A stony pebble of annoyance lodged in her heart at the thought of being stuck the whole summer inside the walls of First Bap, where the bright red carpet made the pews and pulpit look like they floated on a river of blood and there was an elder around every corner wanting to ask how your grades were, like they were gonna tutor you on the spot if you said you were failing.

Sister Butler plunked away at the piano, warming up her fingers. Squeals of laughter came from the back of the church, where the fifth graders were playing some game that consisted of them racing up and down the pews. Never mind that running in the sanctuary was forbidden, ten-year-olds had a way of making the best of being in church.

First Baptist was her second home since she'd moved in with her aunt. Six years ago her, Yola, Kita, and Jalen were the only kids in the whole church. The First Bap Pack, Sister Butler had named them. They all knew what it was like to be the entire choir and youth ministry.

She should have felt closer to them. Honestly, the four of them should hard-core be a clique by now. If five years at Bible study, youth nights, and vacation Bible school didn't make you close to somebody, what did?

Rasheeda was still trying to find out. She liked the First Bap Pack, but calling them friends felt like an exaggeration. Even a lie.

All total, there were twenty kids in the choir now. Most were fifth graders. Sheeda had loved choir and running the then brand-new church's halls when she was that age, too. Now, at thirteen, it wasn't the same. Maybe because they couldn't be all wild like the fifth graders anymore.

Or . . .

She stopped herself from even thinking it. Because she was ready to think "hate" again and if she didn't know anything else, she knew sitting in church thinking about hating was wrong. She mentally blinked the word away and focused on Yola and Kita pretending to be going over the lyrics for today's songs. Sheeda knew they were really looking at the text Jalen had sent to Yola.

Jalen stood on the altos side by himself. Eventually she, Carlos, and Anthony would join him. First it bothered her to be the only girl alto, but whenever she tried singing in a higher voice Sister Butler smiled and said, "All right now, altos gotta alto."

Jalen had his lyric sheet in his hand, lips moving as he read the words—no doubt trying to impress Sister Butler. Sheeda had no idea what Yola saw in him. He had a thick head of wavy hair and skin the shade of coffee that had too much cream in it. It wasn't that he wasn't cute, but he thought he was all that because he got all the leads in the songs and the Christmas play. Pastor's favorite. All the women in the church acted like he was a prize. To them he was a "nice young man." Outside of the view of grown-ups, he was mad cocky. It erased his cuteness.

Sheeda stared past him to the back of the pulpit at the big gold cross. There was a glint to it, like the cross knew she was dreading a summer inside First Baptist and was shining itself on her spirit. She wanted to duck from its presence.

Her Auntie D's voice played like a sermon on demand— *God knows your heart, Luvvie. Can't hide from that.*

The nickname usually had a way of taking the bite off her aunt's constant Scripture quotes and sermons. But lately, there were two Auntie D's—the one who saw that Sheeda meant well and the one giving side-eye as if every little wrong was the world's worst sin. Sheeda never knew which Deandra Tate was going to show up. For sure, the Auntie D who called her "Luvvie," with affection, wasn't around as much.

If she was keeping it a buck, the only time Auntie D was truly happy was when they were at church.

Shocker.

She leaned her head back and sighed toward the ceiling. Her thick rope Marley twists slid on the pew's glossy wood. She adjusted until her neck laid flat. Her phone suddenly glowed beside her. Sheeda glanced at the message: **whatchu doin?** just as Sister Butler clapped her hands. "Okay, let's get started."

Ugh, of course. She couldn't torture the keyboard for three more minutes?

Sheeda made her way into the choir loft. She debated if she had time to answer Dat Boy Ell back. His profile picture, eyes piercing the camera and throwing not one but two middle fingers, made her face even hotter. Middle-finger pic shots in church was most definitely wrong. She didn't need her aunt to tell her that.

His pic wasn't the only thing wrong, though. And since God didn't like a liar, she admitted to herself that her church friendships, a little jealousy, and how she felt about church weren't the only things complicated these days.

Dat Boy Ell was Lennie Jenkins, Mo's older brother. She'd known Lennie since she was eight years old and he was ten. Then he spent so much time being punished for one thing or another that Rasheeda had been afraid of him. Afraid that merely being in his presence might get her in trouble. Especially since Mo's other three brothers were locked up. It took her a while to realize that Lennie only had a big mouth and mainly got in trouble for talking back at school.

That felt forever ago.

He was fifteen now and had never gotten in trouble like his brothers. Him and Mo were the "good" ones, according to her aunt.

Actually she'd said, "Their mother finally caught a break. I *guess* they're the good ones."

Auntie D stayed waiting on people to go wrong.

Anytime her aunt threw shade at Mo and her family, Rasheeda felt two-faced. The only thing that comforted her was her aunt threw shade to pretty much anybody who didn't go to First Bap. She definitely would have never approved of the message Lennie sent commenting on a picture on Rasheeda's FriendMe page: all growed up like... and a GIF of a nearly naked model slo-mo walking down the runway with wind in her weave.

It made Sheeda take a closer look at the picture he was talking about. In it, she wore a white sundress with pink and green flowers. The dress had ruffled straps (three fingers wide, no more, no less), fitted her waist tight then flowed over her wideish hips. She guessed Lennie was referring to the length of the dress. It stopped a few inches above her knee, which was new. Until she'd turned thirteen, every dress she owned came to the middle of her calves.

Sheeda thought it made her look fat. She didn't need help looking thick. But Lennie had liked it. Well, not liked it on her page but at least privately. And the only person in the world she would have shared it with, she couldn't tell.

That had been a few weeks ago. He'd been texting her ever since.

A few times she almost admitted it to Mo. Felt like she should and let Mo say whatever she was going to say because Mo was forever honest. Then that would be that. Only, she still hadn't.

She wasn't worried about Mo getting angry and dramatic. Well, at least not dramatic. Mo was one of the realest people Rasheeda knew. And that was it. Mo could be too honest. Like, pointing-out-your-flaws-to-the-world honest.

Sheeda wasn't sure what truth Mo would tell her once she found out about Lennie, but she knew with all her heart it was one she didn't want to hear.

She glanced at the message, tempted to answer, then shut the screen down and placed the phone in her back pocket.

Sister Butler hit the first note for the song, and Sheeda sang out with all her energy, "Yessss, I'm a believer," hiding behind the lyrics.

MONIQUE

When Ms. Noelle opened La May at the rec center—La Maison de Danse for the bougie at heart—a lot of the older girls in the Cove had joked on it. "What kind of fancy name was Lah May-zon Duh Dance?" They wanted to learn hip-hop or something that would get them on tour or in a music video. And most of them dropped out, with the quickness, when they realized the classes were strictly ballet and jazz.

Until then, Mo had never been in a dance class. That first year Ms. Noelle (Mademoiselle, to her face) forced Mo's body into the craziest most annoying positions. Mo had wanted to quit. Then, one day, they watched a video of Alvin Ailey American Dance Theater and the screen swallowed Mo whole. She was there, in the dark auditorium, watching all those Black bodies move like they didn't have bones.

Ms. Noelle asked, "Who can see themselves doing this?"

And every hand went up. There was a satisfied look on Ms. Noelle's face as she went on to say, "Good. I know that ballet is hard. But its technique is the foundation of modern dance. Want to do that?" She pointed at the screen. "Then you've got to learn ballet."

Monique had been hooked ever since. And good thing, because right about now she felt like her body was ready to break.

"Cambré side."

Monique repeated the word in her head: *calm-BRAY*.

She leaned toward the barre, feeling the stretch in her side.

Knowing the term made her feel like she could go to France and just start talking.

She couldn't, for real, unless everybody around her was going to talk in ballet terms. But when she was in class, it made her feel smarter. Like she'd spent an entire hour in another country.

Every new position change was a command from Ms. Noelle. Yet somehow the words were silky, floating into Mo's ear and slipping through her body so her arms, legs, and torso did the right thing. The tinkling piano music boomed so loud from the speakers, it demanded you follow it. And even though her ballet teacher wasn't yelling, Monique heard her over the music, like it was magic trick.

"Now, back. Cambré." Ms. Noelle held the word out to make sure her tiny class of two understood to stay in the pose.

No cheating. Make the body work, Mo told herself.

She knew she'd never be considered the best dancer. Not as long as her and Mila were competing for the title. Mila was long and lean and looked like the dancers Mo had seen in the ballet videos they watched. Mo was good and she worked hard. Ms. Noelle always praised her for her dedication and how focused she was in class. Mo took the W however she got it.

She couldn't see Mila, but she knew her friend's back was arched as far back as it could go. Mila probably wasn't straining, either. She slid so easily into positions that Mo found herself clenching her teeth to back down the jealousy. In a few days, Mila would be the only person she'd know at the Summer Experience, a ballet intensive they had gotten scholarships to. They needed each other.

Her back straining in the deep arch, Mo gripped the barre, loosened her jaw.

How in the world did Mila look like she could stay leaned back like this all day?

She exhaled slowly through her mouth, feeling the tension in her spine. Seriously, it felt like it was going to crack.

Books by
PAULA CHASE

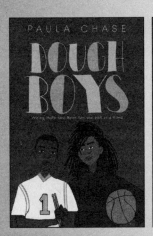

Greenwillow Books
An Imprint of HarperCollinsPublishers

www.harpercollinschildrens.com